GINO'S REVENGE: MY JOY PART 2

CHRISTIAN CASHELLE

DYNAMIC IMAGE PUBLICATIONS

ISBN: 0-9894423-3-0
ISBN-13: 978-0-9894423-3-6

To you,
At times, when you are dead set on revenge, make sure you
are not the one who has done wrong.

Prologue

"Today we won't mourn the death of this earthly being, but we shall celebrate his life. Let us all remember the good times, and rejoice that another soul has made it out of this hateful world. Let us not cry for his demise, but pray for his eternal rest. We all have our crosses to bear, so let our judgmental hearts take heed at what we believe to be true."

Silence lay across the eerie gravesite as the Reverend spoke loosely of someone he was sure not to have known. Deceived loved ones, oblivious to the lifestyle of their fallen soldier, shed alligator tears and nodded their heads, hanging on to every word that was spoken. Enemies as well as friends looked on as the coffin was prepared for its six-foot flight into the soil by the hired men and women dressed in black, showing no emotion on their professional faces.

Camryn's face grew stone-like as the funeral coordinator began to lower the casket into the cold ground.

"Ashes to ashes, dust to dust."

Camryn wondered if her unborn son knew that his father was lying lifeless in front of them. Maybe he knew that he would never meet the Gino that cared about them. Camryn cried at the thought.

Camryn looked to the front row to see Gino's grandmother sitting next to Tameka, who had been crying her eyes out the whole funeral. She wasn't loud or ignorant with her cry, but Camryn could tell that some underlying pain was hiding in Tameka's cries.

All Camryn knew was that she wasn't a part of it and didn't need to be. As the casket lowered, Camryn prayed that God would have mercy on Gino. She wasn't one to judge, but she sure didn't think that his resume was squeaky clean either.

"Goodbye, Gino," Camryn whispered as she pressed her hands to her belly through her coat.

Camryn wasn't sure if it was because of her pushing on her ninth month of pregnancy, or if she was really sad, but she cried as they lowered Gino's casket into the ground. Camryn cried hard. Almost as hard as she'd cried when the ten o'clock news reported they had found the body of a local notorious drug dealer in his car in a vacant parking lot.

She didn't understand. Yes, he had forewarned her but why now? Why when he was attempting to make a connection with her and their son? Why would he wait until he knew something was wrong before trying to resolve things?

Camryn was scared. Before, it was a choice of letting her son know his father or not. Now she didn't have that choice.

She had to get out of this city.

She tried to hurry and leave the cemetery once the service was dismissed. She didn't want to talk to anyone, and sure didn't want anyone to see that she was pregnant and just about due. She didn't even know if his friends and family knew she existed outside of the ones she knew.

"Camryn!"

She froze as her name was called out by Tameka. She inhaled before turning around. Tameka was walking with her arm around Gino's grandmother. Camryn didn't speak when they stopped in front of her.

"Is this my great-grandson?" his grandmother said, reaching out and placing her hand on the tip of Camryn's belly. Startled, Camryn lost her footing but Tameka held her up.

"Are you okay?" Tameka asked. Camryn looked at her as if she had a third eye. She straightened herself up and nodded. "It's okay," Tameka said.

"Are you coming to the repass?" she said. Camryn shook her head no.

"No ma'am, I have to get home to check on my grandmother," Camryn said. She nodded before Tameka told her she would meet her at the car.

"We need to talk," Tameka said.

"Why?" Camryn said, ready to put Tameka, and all that came with her, behind her.

"Can you meet me somewhere?" Tameka asked, ignoring Camryn's question.

"Tameka, I-"

"It's really important."

Camryn looked at Tameka and could tell that she couldn't say much in their current location. She rolled her eyes and sighed.

"Fine."

"Meet me at the mall in front of the post office in two hours," Tameka said. Camryn nodded as Tameka jogged to catch up with Gino's grandmother.

Camryn sat on the bench in front of the mall's post office with both of her hands around her belly. Lately, her stomach had been getting tight, and her doctor had warned that meant her son was coming soon.

Now that it was about a month away, Camryn had to admit she would be glad to have him here, because it seemed as if she had been pregnant for too long. She knew that was because of all the added drama though. She wasn't as nervous as she thought she would be to go through the actually labor, but she figured she would be in the few weeks to come.

She peered over the Chanel glasses that Gino had given her, before the whole pregnancy, to see if she could spot Tameka anywhere. Camryn had been a little late for the impromptu meeting, but Tameka hadn't shown yet either.

Camryn was getting impatient. She didn't even want to come, and her back had been aching since she left the cemetery. Right when she was about to leave, Tameka slid onto the bench next to her.

"What do we need to talk about?" Camryn said as soon as Tameka sat down.

"When are you due?" Tameka asked.

"Late next month, why?"

"Gino left us a going away present," Tameka said, smirking.

"What do you mean, he left us?" Camryn asked. Tameka smacked her lips.

"You ask a lot of questions, just listen dang," Tameka said. She pulled a small key from her pocket and held it *out in front of Camryn. Camryn took it and read the number on the key. She was confused, but didn't say anything.*

"That key goes to a box in there," Tameka said, pointing to the clear doors of the post office. "There's something in there for you, but you need to get it before the police do."

"Hold on," Camryn said, but Tameka shook her head.

"It's nothing like that," Tameka said. Camryn sighed before looking at Tameka.

"What happened to him?" Camryn asked. Tameka turned and looked at her for a second before turning back.

"I'm sure you saw the news," Tameka whispered.

"No, Tameka, what really happened to him?"

They stared each other down for a few seconds before Tameka looked away. Camryn could see the hurt and guilt in her eyes.

"Let's just move on with our lives," Tameka said, standing up. "We don't have to see each other anymore. You won't hear from me or anyone else. Gino's grandmother promised to take it to her grave. We're free now.

"Oh, and don't open it in the post office," she added. "Take it to your car."

She walked away without another word. Camryn sat on the bench for about ten minutes before getting up and walking into the post office. Her heart rate sped up as she searched among the wall of boxes and found Box 459. Sliding the old key into the hole, Camryn pulled out the small black purse, closed the box and made her way quickly out of the post office.

Once she got to her car, she started it but kept it in park, her curiosity killing her.

"Jesus," she yelled as she unzipped the bag to see crisp one hundred dollar bills stacked together. There was so many that she couldn't even phantom how much was in the purse. She couldn't breathe. She didn't know what to do, until she saw the small note attached to the first stack:

250 stacks. Consider this child support.

ONE

Granny Watson sighed as she looked through the torn photo album of her family. So many happy memories of her only child's birth and the birth of her grandsons. Every birthday, milestone, and big moment had been captured by her old, trusty camera and cemented into these laminated pages kept comfortably in a drawer near her bed.

It pained her, however, that with all the happy memories, so many sad ones remained. There were only two of them left now; Granny Watson and one of her grandsons.

It had been a few months since Gino's funeral, and her world felt numb. When she got the call from Tameka that there had been a shooting at their home, Granny Watson just knew that her baby would be okay. Surely, she hadn't done anything THAT bad for God to take another one of her loves home before her. She had already seen her own child's demise....when would it end?

She had been good at keeping her children's secrets, but she was tired. It was exhausting how much she had to pray and fast; and now she was beginning to believe that her labor hadn't been enough. Somehow, she'd still lost them.

Her one remaining joy was her surviving grandson, but even she could see the wheels turning over his twin's murder.

April, Granny Watson's only daughter, was just 20 when she birthed her twin sons, Gino and Jean. Their father had been like a menstrual cycle, in Granny Watson's words. He only seemed to come around once a month and every time he seemed to cause April to bleed. Granny Watson didn't want to run April into his arms even more, so she didn't voice her opinion until it was too late.

The boys were only 12 when April was killed and their father was charged with her murder.

Granny Watson kept them close, but it always seemed as if Gino kept his eyes on bigger things. He was always finding ways to make his own money so that Granny Watson didn't have to support his social habits. Jean was more into books. He wasn't focused in school, but he read books about history, black inventors, culture and other things. He always wanted to learn in that way.

She smiled as she remembered when they were just becoming teenagers and finally started showing signs of life after their mother's death. They decided to open a business together but couldn't agree on what to sale. They'd been back and forth from cutting grass, selling mixed CDs, washing cars...you name it. Finally, Gino ended the discussion.

"Bro, you figure it out. I can sell anything."

And that seemed to be their little system all through high school: Jean thought of the plan. Gino executed the plan.

Granny Watson's proudest day was seeing those boys graduate from high school, but it was Jean's saddest. Gino had set his sights on an illegal business in the city. He tried to get Jean to come with him, but Jean wasn't leaving Granny Watson. He never did. He'd told Gino that because of his photophobia being so severe, he wouldn't move. His sensitivity to light hadn't gotten any worse, but they all accepted his excuse.

Granny Watson couldn't talk Gino out of his plan. She was scared for his life all the time, but it seemed as if every time he came back home, he had a story of success to tell them. When he started talking about Tameka, Granny Watson could feel the bad energy, but as always...she kept it to herself. Jean had figured it out though, and tried to save his brother as best as he could.

She tried to shake those thoughts from her head, but as she watched her only grandson sit with newspaper clippings of his twin's death, Tati's trial, and everything else that had transpired, she knew that this was far from over.

And she could do nothing to stop it.

Something wasn't adding up about his twin's death and for the last few weeks he had been trying to figure out what it was. The guilt of not attending his funeral and the hatred for whoever pulled the trigger fueled his investigation and it seemed like that flame grew by the day.

Jean didn't buy the story that Twan's girlfriend, Tati, also known as Baby, killed Gino after watching him shoot down Twan. He didn't believe that Tameka was too caught up in the shoot out that she didn't see Baby pick up the gun. He didn't believe that if Gino knew Twan was betraying him, that he would have let him in his home that night. Nothing was making sense to Jean, and that usually meant that it wasn't the truth.

His mind just worked in that way.

He knew the last time that his brother was home that something wasn't right. He could tell in the way that he talked about his unborn child and everything that was going on. Gino knew he was about to die, but he refused to hear Jean when he suggested Gino stay.

He wasn't running from anything or anyone.

Now his brother was gone, he didn't know why and most importantly, he didn't know where his nephew was. Jean needed answers and he was determined to find out exactly what he wanted to know.

Gino never let anything done to him slide. Revenge was second nature for him and Jean believed in it wholeheartedly. He'd find out who was really responsible for his twin's death and make sure they paid for it. Then he'd find Camryn and the baby. After all, they were family.

Most of his plan would be on the fly, but he knew where he needed to start. Nothing that made sense about this all had something in common.

Tameka.

TWO

Baywood looked around the peaceful block and sighed in content. Things had been rough for the last couple of months. Some people were hurt by Gino and Twan's death and others were just upset that Baywood and Chase were now in charge. He learned a long time ago that he couldn't please everybody and he didn't plan on starting now.

So he and Chase developed a system, similar to Gino's so the majority of the team would be comfortable with it. They changed it enough to make it their own.

Baywood and Chase were different from Gino and Twan. Baywood was simple and didn't try to live above his means. Chase was all about being able to take care of Lori, his twins and unborn baby…and stay out of jail. They were both low key bosses. They didn't want to micro manage like Gino did, but that meant they had to trust the team completely.

They reduced their cash houses from four to two and cut down on the number of block captains. "So far, so good." Baywood thought.

"I'm about to head out," Chase said, knocking Baywood out of his thoughts. "Gotta see my mean girl before I have to induce her labor early."

Baywood laughed. "Aight, I'll catch you tomorrow."

"I'll be around, mayne."

Chase drove through the neighborhood, nodding to a few people who showed him love. It had been almost two years since his release, but after being locked up for nearly three years he was still grateful everyday that he was out.

He was most grateful for his family. Lori was pregnant with the twins when he took his gun charge. The only thing he regretted was not being there when they were born. Lori stayed down for him, no matter what people said. Now with them being a few months away from having another baby, Chase was determined to do right this time around.

When he walked into his three-bedroom home, his twins were terrorizing Lori, who was stretched out on the couch with a frown on her face.

"Why you so tired?" Jacob asked his mother.

"Because your brother is going to be a soccer player."

Chase laughed, which made all three of them look up. Lori closed her eyes in relief as the twins took off towards their father.

"It's bedtime."

"They wanted you to tuck them in."

"Um hum, you just being lazy, Baby Momma."

"Hey! I gave them a bath!" Lori defended herself. "That's the best I can do."

Chase laughed before taking the twins upstairs and putting them in their separate rooms. He wondered how Jacob would react to having to share his room soon and asked Lori what she thought when he got back downstairs.

"He's so happy about it being a boy that he probably hasn't realized yet."

Chase looked at her for a moment and frowned. "What's wrong? Why you sound depressed?"

Lori sighed. "I'm not depressed, but I miss Meka." Chase sucked his teeth. "Stop baby. I know you didn't like her, but she was the only friend I had."

Chase chuckled. "Not my fault you mean as hell."

"I'm done talking to you," Lori said. Chase laughed as Lori struggled to get up. Chase waited a second before pulling her back to his chest.

"Chill out…It's been almost a year, Lo," Chase said. "I know that's your girl, but she ain't thinking about nothing from here. You gon have to find some new friends. I'm your best friend anyway."

That made Lori smile and kiss him.

"You're right. Your plate is in the microwave, best friend." Lori laughed as Chase playfully pushed her onto the couch and took off towards the kitchen. She saw his phone light up and Baywood's name flash across the screen.

"Chase, your phone!"

"Who is it?"

"Wood."

"He don't want nothing." Lori sat back on the couch but Baywood called right back. This time Chase heard it. "Answer it!" Lori rolled her eyes before plucking if off the table.

"What's up, Wood? Chase is eating."

"Ay, are the kids sleep?" he asked.

"Yeah, why? What's wrong?" Lori asked, sitting up.

"Open the door. I got somebody with me y'all need to see."

"So you're Gino's twin?"

Jean nodded slowly as he looked at the three of their faces. Each was looking at him as if he had stepped out of the grave.

"Why we never heard of you?"

"How we know you telling the truth?" Lori asked. Chase sucked his teeth.

"That's stupid, bae. They pretty much identical."

"I look better," Jean said, speaking for the first time. Chase and Lori laughed. Baywood, who had been in shock since Jean approached him at the diner an hour ago, just looked on in silence. Jean side-eyed him before smiling.

"The reason you haven't heard of me is because I was on a need to know basis."

"Yea? So why we need to know you now?" Baywood asked. Jean lifted his hands.

"Not here to shake nothing up. Just need a few things cleared up about my brother's death."

Chase and Baywood nodded in understanding, but Lori nervously cleared her throat.

"What do you mean? Baby killed him and now she's in jail."

Jean looked at her for a second. "Yeah, that's the story…"

"…So what you want us to do?" Baywood asked.

"I need help finding two people."

"Who?" Chase asked, but Lori already knew. She kept her mouth closed, but held onto her belly as Jean looked back at her with a smirk on his face.

"Tameka and Camryn."

Lori offered Jean and Baywood a plate. Chase was into whatever highlights ESPN was playing while Lori busied herself with cleaning the kitchen and trying to listen to Baywood and Jean without them noticing.

There were only a few noticeable differences. He was a little smaller, but still muscular. Gino wore his face clean shaven, but Jean had a very neat and low cut beard and mustache.

It was clear that he was Gino's twin. Lori just hoped he wasn't like him in other ways.

She didn't know the details of what happened that night, but she knew the story never sat right with her. She never understood why Tameka had to leave and why she couldn't tell Lori where she was going.

Lori only had a number that Tameka would call her from to check on her and the kids, but she was hoping to keep that bit of information to herself.

"So where you staying at?" Baywood asked.

"The Hyatt on Main," Jean said. Baywood nodded.

"Well, G was my brother, so anything I can do let me know."

"I appreciate that. First I gotta deal with the house."

"I thought that was in Tameka's name?" Lori blurted. Both of them glanced at her.

"…It was in our grandmother's name. She transferred it to me so I could sell it."

"…Oh," Lori mumbled. She decided to excuse herself and go sit with her man in the living room before she said too much. "Did the Seahawks win?"

"Yeah."

"…Babe, what do you think he wants?"

Chase shrugged. "I don't really care."

For the next couple of days, everyone on the blocks welcomed Jean as if they'd known Gino had an identical twin all along. Even people who couldn't stand Gino were acting as if they'd been the best of friends. He walked around with shades on all the time but Lori felt like he was always looking at her when she was around.

Lori was trying not to stress the situation. This pregnancy was very high risk. Not long after Tameka left, Lori had a miscarriage. She wasn't trying to get pregnant again, but Chase was determined. It was only a few months before he succeeded. They were six months in and all seemed to be going smoothly. Lori wasn't going to let whatever mess Tameka had done disrupt what she and Chase had going on.

Lori jumped when her cell phone rang.

"Hey best friend," Tameka said.

"You got a problem," Lori whispered, even though the kids were sleep and Chase was gone. Tameka laughed.

"What? You trying to go into early labor?"

"If dead nigga's identical twins keep popping up in town, I just might."

"…What are you talking about?"

"Does the name Jean ring a bell?"

"Lori say what you mean."

"Your dead husband has an identical twin that is in town and looking for his sister-in-law."

Tameka laughed, hard. "Be for real. Gino doesn't have any family besides his granny. I was with him over eight years. I would know."

"Antt! Wrong! He's very real, very here, and very upset about not knowing what really happened to his twin."

"Baby shot him," Tameka said quickly. "We know what happened. I know what I saw. I was there!"

"That's why he wants to talk to you," Lori said, getting annoyed with her best friend. There was definitely more to the story than Tameka wanted to admit. Lori just didn't care at this point.

"Whatever, he doesn't need to talk to me about anything. It's been almost a year. He needs to let it go."

"Yeah, okay. I gotta go. Call me later."

"Lori, nobody knows you're talking to me."

"Bye Meka." Lori hung up before Tameka could respond. "I don't have time for this."

"Time for what?"

Lori jumped to see Chase, Baywood, and Jean walking in the kitchen. She held her chest with one hand and her belly with the other.

"Really Chase? You trying to kill me?"

Baywood laughed. "Shorty, I'm sure it'll take more than that."

"Ha, ha." Lori hit him in his arm. Chase put his hand on the back of Lori's neck and pulled her in for a kiss.

"We need to talk for a minute," he said as Baywood and Jean sat at the table. Lori nodded and quickly made her exit. While she was walking upstairs, she took her phone out of her pocket and erased the number Tameka called her from.

"So some of the squad is worried about what you being here means," Baywood said.

"Like if you trying to come back and claim your brother's place," Chase said. "We got a smooth little system going on and…"

"I'm hip," Jean said, cutting him off. "Everything running smoothly. I ain't trying to jump in that. That was G's life. I'm just trying to figure out why it ended."

"Right…" Chase said. "Well, nobody knows where Baby's people are, but I got a connect that can get you in to see her."

"Good looking," Jean said. "How far is it from here?"

"About three hours."

"You need us to roll with you?" Baywood asked. Jean caught Chase side-eye him. He made a mental note that Chase was going to be a problem and that he'd have to keep his eye on him.

"Nah," he smiled. "Just set it up. I'll handle the rest."

Jean relaxed in the driver's seat of his rented Ford truck while he sat at the gas pump waiting for it to fill up. The sun was shining and for it to be early November, the weather wasn't half bad. Jean smirked as he noticed a woman at her own car eyeing him. He knew word had gotten out that Gino's twin was in town and that seemed to bring him a lot of female attention. He probably would have entertained her if he wasn't on the phone with Granny Watson.

"You aren't supposed to pump gas and talk on a cellular phone at the same time."

Jean chuckled. "That's what you're worried about right now?"

"Don't sass me."

He smiled. "Yes ma'am. How you feeling?"

"My knee is a little dull from that dance class I went to with those old ladies."

"Ma, how you callin' them old, but your knee hurt?"

"'Cause I can and they are! I'm about to be done talking to you."

Jean laughed. "I'm sorry. I'm done."

"So you going alone?"

"Best way to get things done."

Granny Watson sighed. "Just be careful. I'm still not okay with this."

"You want to know where your great-grandson is don't you?"

"...Just be careful."

"I will. Talk to you later."

Jean got out of the car and replaced the fuel nozzle on the hook. After tightening his gas cap, he got back into the truck and put the address to the correctional facility into his GPS.

As he rode through the small town, he thought of all the stories his brother told him about his empire. Jean could map them out in his head now that he'd been around for a couple of weeks. He had been laying low, surveying everything, but now it was time to put his plan into action.

Jean had people to find and answers to get. He was hoping to get Baby in on his plan, but he wasn't sure if she'd accept what he had to offer her. He'd heard that she had been very loyal to Twan in the time that they were together and she was apparently the only woman that Twan ever allowed to be seen publicly with him.

Jean had a strong feeling that Baby wouldn't be too quick to help him avenge his brother's death but she would want revenge for Twan's. He could pretty much bet on that.

Jean was confident, he and Gino definitely shared that trait. He just went about what he wanted a different way.

Jean knew all about Twan from Gino's stories of his best friend. He handled all of Gino's dirty work and kept all of his secrets. Gino used to be concerned about Twan never relaxing or doing anything other than help him run the business. That was until Baby came into the picture.

She had a history of drama and Gino was skeptical of her interest in Twan. As time passed, Jean could tell that Baby kind of won them all over.

He couldn't figure out how Baby ended up taking the fall for his brother's murder. He didn't know if Twan or Tameka was behind it. Baby seemed very loyal to Twan. Jean was hoping that she still was. She may not be able to tell him where Tameka was, but he had a feeling he knew who could. All he needed Baby to do was tell him what happened the night Twan and Gino were shot.

Jean was about an hour into his drive when he thought about his nephew. He wondered what he looked like, where they were staying, and if his mother planned on telling him who his father was.

He became angry as he thought about the possibility of never seeing him, or Granny Watson never seeing him. Jean had to make sure that didn't happen.

His cell phone vibrated in his pocket. Keeping his eyes on the road, he pulled it out and answered. Jean knew it could only be one of two people and Granny Watson had already called.

"What up, punk."

The caller sucked her teeth. "I told you about being rude."

Jean laughed. "What you want, Rem?"

"Nothing now, jerk."

"Woman chill, I'm playing."

"That's all you do. It's like everyday is get on Remy's nerves day for you."

Remy Hightower was Gino and Jean's godsister. Her mom was their mom's best friend while April was dealing with their abusive father. Remy was a few year's younger so the twins took their big brother roles seriously. Nobody was good enough, but Remy was no angel. She didn't make their self-appointed jobs easy.

"When you coming back?" she asked, or more like whined. Ever since Gino's funeral, Remy had been very clingy. Jean knew that Remy could tell he had been plotting revenge ever since Granny Watson got the call from Tameka. He couldn't even bring himself to go to his own twin's funeral. He promised himself once everything was settled that he'd go tell him the good news in person. So he could rest in peace. "Hello!" Remy yelled.

"Shut up. I already told you when I was coming home."

Remy sucked her teeth again. "You didn't! All you said was when I'm done."

"There's your answer…and you're the one they sent to college." he said, laughing at his own joke.

"… I really don't like you. Be careful."

"You like me enough. Call you later."

"Bye jerk!"

Jean thought about calling her back to bother her, but decided on focusing on the mission at hand instead.

It only took him two and half hours to get to the correctional facility. As soon as he pulled into the parking lot, Baywood called.

"Jenny said she saw you pull up. Wait ten minutes before going in."

Jean frowned. "How she see me?"

"She's in the yard near the fence."

Jean looked around and saw the yard. All he could see was a sea of orange and blue jumpsuits, until he spotted a tall, lanky officer standing near the fence, looking his way.

"Alright, 'preciate it."

"No doubt."

Jean could tell why Gino had Baywood as third in command. Should have been him at second instead of Twan. Jean watched as Jenny began to usher the inmates back into the building with the help of another officer. Jails always reminded him of his dad and what he did to wind up in prison for the rest of his life.

Since he was related to the victim that Baby was convicted of killing, Jean had to assume a fake identity for this visit. He pulled out the ID and locked everything else in the car. Jenny came up to the front desk, checked Jean in, and took him back to the visitation room. Jenny pointed to a table in the back. She already had Baby sitting there.

"No more than thirty minutes before I have to get her back."

Jean nodded before Jenny sat down at an empty post.

Baby's dark hair was in a long, sleek ponytail that started at the back of her head. Even from behind Jean could tell that her jumpsuit did her body no justice.

He walked around the table and sat down, trying not to laugh at the frozen look on her face.

"...I watched you die."

"Sometimes our eyes deceive us."

"Nah...nah. I wouldn't be in here for something I ain't do. I watched you die."

Jean eyed her for a second. "You watched my twin die."

Baby's eyebrow rose. "Twin. As in identical twin?" Jean nodded. "Why no one heard of you?"

"Family secret," Jean smirked.

Baby sat back and laughed hard. "Wow...a twin."

"You done?"

"What you want with me, Gino's twin? Trying to kill me?"

"You breathing ain't you?"

"Look...I don't know what you want," Baby started while standing up. Jean's jaw tightened.

"Sit down."

Baby quickly did as told, not excited about his cold, demanding tone.

"Tell me what happened that night."

"To do that, I'd have to tell you how that night came to pass."

"Start talking."

"For what?"

Jean frowned. "For what? You really trying to serve a bid for something you ain't do?"

Baby leaned over the table with a frown on her face. "It look like I'm in here for fun? I already been charged!"

"Ever heard of an appeal?"

Baby sat back, chewing on her bottom lip. "You can get me out of here?"

"Tell me what happened and where I can find Tameka."

Baby folded her arms. "I look stupid? You don't get both until you prove your word."

Jean smirked. "I already got a little plug for you in here. Tell me what I need to know and I'll have you out by summer."

"I'll tell you what happened that night and when you get me out of here…I'll give you a front row, private viewing of Tameka's funeral."

Jean licked his lips as he watched Baby hold her left hand out across the table. She smiled when his right hand joined it.

"So what type of connect you have in here?" Baby asked.

"Just keeping your books stacked and someone looking out for you," Jean said. Baby looked at him and nodded.

"I didn't like your brother."

"…Is that relevant?"

"Yeah…everyone was sold on him being the street Jesus, but I saw through it. I was used to everyone drooling over how everything looked," Baby picked at her nails. "They ain't ever worried about the work it takes to get it."

"Which is why you wanted Twan."

Baby nodded. "I saw everything he did for Gino. All the bodies he dropped, yet he stood back and let Gino have all the shine. That took control and strength. Gino didn't deserve his loyalty."

"That's not your place to say," Jean said with a tight jaw.

"As his woman it was. Gino didn't see him at night like I did. All the stress and regret from doing everything Gino wanted. I started hating Gino for making Twan so loyal to him….so that's when I came up wit the plan."

"To kill him?" he asked, tempted to hop over the table and choke her.

"No," Baby said, shaking her head. "To take the business."

Baby looked at Jean to see if he wanted her to continue.

"I'm listening."

"Twan wasn't the only unhappy and underpaid worker in the camp. Most people were just too scared. I knew Baywood and Chase would never out Gino, so we started small in the chain and got a few workers on our side. Everything was smooth, until I messed up." Baby looked down and wiped a tear. "I'm the reason Twan is dead."

"Did you shoot him?"

Baby shook her head. "Tameka did."

Jean looked shocked. "How that happen?"

"After the wedding, Meka was still hurt by Gino getting that little girl pregnant and I could tell. So I tried to get her on our side, only she'd already figured out Twan was the snake. I wanted her to work with us, but she had her own plan."

Jean felt his blood boiling. Baby was slowly confirming everything he already believed.

"Who shot my brother?"

"Twan did. Meka staged it to look like they had me tied up to get Twan to the house. Twan and Gino started arguing and soon shots were fired. Tameka said she wanted G dead, but I guess when she saw him fall….she had a change of heart," Baby began crying. "She wasn't supposed to shoot him! He did everything she asked and she shot him in front of me!" Baby gritted her teeth. "I was tied up! I couldn't do anything! When the police got there, she told them Gino shot Twan and I shot him because of it."

"But weren't you still tied up?"

Baby laughed while shaking her head. "She said she was able to restrain me because she feared for her life."

"Should she?"

Baby nodded. "Get me out of here and she's as good as gone."

THREE

"I can't see you!"

"Nana, you have to turn the camera on."

"Do what? This is stupid."

Camryn giggled. "Well, if you want to see your baby, you're going to have to figure it out."

Miss Marie groaned. "Hold on, let me find one of these kids runnin' round here."

Camryn laughed while looking at Ian, who was sitting next to her looking around to see where Nana's voice was coming from.

"Your Nana is silly," Camryn said. She was lying on her stomach, so she leaned over and kissed Ian's chubby cheek. His giggle would never cease to amaze her. It always felt like a good cup of tea warming her insides.

She played with him as he played with his toes. She could hear Nana fussing at one of her great nephews to help her work the video chat app. Camryn clapped when she finally saw Nana's face.

"That's my diva," Cam said. Nana waved her off.

"What happened to old fashion letters?" Nana asked.

"Then you wouldn't be able to see this handsome face!" Camryn put Ian in between her arms and held the phone out in front of him. "Say, Hi Nana!"

"Aw, look at you, little handsome man! I miss you guys."

"We miss you, too," Cam said. "But only two more months until someone's birthday! Can you believe it?"

"No, I can't believe he's almost one. This year flew by!"

Cam smiled while looking down at Ian. It was a very rocky year, but one well worth it. Cam and Nana talked until Ian went down for his nap. Cam promised to call her later before going to take a shower. She had a lot of things to get down before he woke up.

Camryn Lacey was only 21 and had to remind herself daily. After fighting for her and her son's life while pregnant, it was no wonder that she had matured beyond her years. A lot had changed since she moved and started on her sociology degree. One thing that would always and forever be consistent was the fact that Ian Mikel Lacey was her first priority.

She played with her freshly cut bob in the mirror and thought about letting Mia touch-up her caramel highlights. Her mind wandered off to her son's father as it seemed to at the most random and inappropriate times. Camryn had no idea why their fiery romance had been on her mind lately, but she took comfort in the fact that she seemed to only envision the good times in her recent dreams.

Flashback 2005

17-year-old Camryn rolled her eyes playfully as she moved her heavy backpack to her right shoulder. She was walking down the street from the bus stop, hoping she could have enough for a car soon, when the same black Ford truck that had been following her for the last week rolled up on the side of her.

"Good afternoon, Miss Camryn."

"Your business must be slow," Cam said, trying not to stare at his fresh lining or his smile.

"Why you say that?"

"'Cause you always bothering me."

Gino laughed hard. "Come ride with me." Cam stopped and glared at him with her hand on her hip. Gino lifted his left hand up. "Not like that, little momma! Just trying to feed you. I know you don't eat that nasty cafeteria food."

Cam looked at him for a minute before her stomach forced her feet to walk around and climb into the truck.

Gino smiled victoriously. "I knew you were a smart girl."

She laughed."Whatever. I want Culver's."

Cam waited until they had their food and were seated at a booth in the back before she began to grill him.

"So what's the deal? Why you been stalking me?"

Gino laughed while looking at her in awe. "You know who I am?" Cam nodded. "Well, that usually makes girls a little more friendly."

Cam sat back in the booth and smirked. "Why? Because my age or your status?"

"Mostly because I'm so handsome," he said with a cocky grin. They both laughed and even though Cam shook her head as if she wasn't affected, that was the moment Gino pulled her straight into his world.

She still cried for him. No matter how everyone around her chose to remember him, Cam chose the last time they spoke. The night he was murdered.

The car ride was silent. Gino was taking Camryn back to Denny's to get her car and then following her to Mia's to make sure that she got there.

Gino had gotten a text from his wife saying she figured out who the snake was and had proof. He had to get home so he could take care of this once and for all.

Camryn thanked him when he pulled up next to her car. Before she could get out, Gino locked the door.

"Gino, look," she panicked.

"Camryn, just listen to me for a minute," he said, beginning to get frustrated with her. He knew that he had caused her a lot of pain but he didn't want her to be scared of him.

Gino waited until Camryn sat back and sighed.

"I've done a lot wrong, Camryn, and I can honestly say I only regret one thing," he said looking directly at her. She batted her eyelashes and tears glossed her eyes.

"Gino, don't do this," Camryn said. He pulled her hand to make her look at him.

"I'm sorry I did this to you. I messed up your life. You are so much more than I gave your credit for," Gino said.

"G, I'm over it," Camryn said, trying to pull away.

"But I'm not. Camryn, you were right that day at your house when you said I loved you. I love you. And my son."

Camryn broke down and told Gino that she hated him for what had happened to her in the last eight months.

"You've been going to that church with your grandmother, right?" Gino asked. Camryn sniffed and nodded. "What does your pastor say about forgiveness?"

"He says that we have to forgive others because God forgave us. And if He forgave us, who are we to hold grudges on someone else." Camryn mumbled, wiping her face with her hands. "That holding grudges keeps us from having blessed lives."

"Camryn I'm sorry, but I'm sure that now is that time for you to live," Gino said, putting both of his hands on Camryn's belly. He looked down at it for a second because their son was kicking. "Something bad is going to happen to me. I don't know what is going on but I need you to forgive me and live your life."

"G, what's going on?" Camryn said.

"Promise me," Gino said, slightly shaking Camryn's arms. She nodded while trying not to cry.

Dwelling on his death was not helping her raise her son or move on with her life. However, their connection had been instant. She couldn't shake it if she tried. Cam had committed herself to him, even knowing he was still dealing with Tameka.

Looking back, Cam felt that she was the cause of everything that happened. If she would have just listened to Mia, she wouldn't have almost died twice. But then she wouldn't have Ian either.

Cam cleaned her apartment as quickly as she could. She was running dish water when Ian's soft cries floated through their home. Cam sighed before turning the water off and going to get him.

"Almost finished," she said, taking him into the living room to his playpen. When she tried to walk away, he cried harder.

Cam sighed and picked him back up. She heard a key in the door and smiled down at Ian.

"Titi's here!"

Mia came through the door, instantly smiling.

"Hey handsome!"

"Say hey Titi! Keep me company while Mommy does dishes!"

"Come here," Mia said, taking Ian from Cam. He immediately laid his head on her chest and pulled her hair.

Cam smirked. "Just like his daddy."

"Ew!" Mia frowned. Cam laughed as she went back to the dishes.

"How's the new job going?"

"Pretty good," Mia said. "Today was stressful, but Jay brought me lunch."

"Aw, what a boyfriend," Cam teased.

"Speaking of…have you talked to my cousin."

"…"

"He said he's been trying to call you."

"Jayson and I have nothing to talk about."

Mia sucked her teeth. "Camryn Charmaine."

"What? He's the one that left."

Mia remained quiet. Although she didn't want to get between her cousin and her best friend, she wanted to help them get back together.

Jayson was the first guy Cam got involved with after Gino. They flirted and got to know each other while Cam was pregnant but didn't begin to date exclusively until Ian was two months. Everything was great until about a month ago when Jayson accepted a job on the east coast to manage part of the company he worked for. She was happy for him, but it seemed a little too easy for him to leave her. It was as if they hadn't been involved at all.

Cam was tired of dealing with men who thought leaving was the best option.

She sighed and finished up the dishes before going back into the living room with Mia and Ian. They were watching television and for a ten-month-old, Ian was very alert and attentive. Mia looked like she was almost sleep.

They ordered in and sat around until Ian got sleepy.

"Let me get him ready for bed," Cam said, picking Ian up and cuddling him. Mia stood up and sighed.

"Yeah, I'm going to head out. Jeremiah just texted that he's on his way. He got off early."

"Behave ma'am," Cam said, walking towards the back and looking over her shoulder.

Mia laughed too. "I'll lock the door on my way out."

Cam sighed as she pulled Ian's clothes off. "Let's make you the freshest smelling baby again!" she said, kissing his belly. He giggled and clapped both of his hands against her face. She smiled before running his water and putting him in the tub. He only had a few toys since she was very cautious about bath time. Cam got lost in her own thoughts until he started splashing her with water and whining. That's when she knew it was time for bed.

Within twenty minutes she had him dressed and in his crib. Cam looked down at him as he tried to find a comfortable spot and couldn't help but think about his father. Although he had her color, Ian was every bit of Gino. Sometimes that made Cam feel good and sometimes it scared her to death. She tried not to think about it too much, but she was constantly praying that Gino's wicked ways were not a generational curse. She didn't go through a life-threatening pregnancy to have to deal with him acting like his father in ten plus years.

"Jesus, help me," Cam said with a smirk, leaning over to kiss his forehead. She made sure the monitor was on and headed to her own bed. Her phone was ringing when she walked in.

Cam groaned in irritation before picking it up. "Yes, Jayson."

"You finally figured out how to work your phone?"

"It's called do not disturb. What do you want?"

"Camryn, you really about to do this? Talk to me better than that, baby."

She sighed. "I'm not going to argue with you. You made your choice."

"So I can't miss you?" he asked, cutting her off. "You don't miss me?"

Cam pulled her comforter back and looked around for her remote control. She did miss him the first few days, but crying over it wouldn't solve anything.

"What good would that do us?"

Jayson laughed a little. "That's cool, momma. I'll talk to you some other time."

"…Yeah."

FOUR

Baywood rubbed his tired eyes as his alarm went off, letting him know that it was six in the morning. He could tell it was still dark outside, because no light came through his bedroom shades. He contemplated staying in the bed next to his woman, but he had to get his day started.

Baywood left the door open to his bathroom as he took a shower so he could see the body that lay in his bed. He smirked thinking of a few hours ago when he finally got to spend some time with his woman. Between her working and his hustling, they didn't get to see each other much. They were okay though, always had been.

Baywood had been with Tina since they were younger. He didn't have time to play around and mess with random girls. He was about Tina and his money. They didn't have any kids and weren't looking to have any, so that gave them reason to work as much as they did. Tina didn't bother him about hustling, but he knew that she wasn't particularly fond of it, so she stayed away. Baywood even thought after they got married three years ago, that she'd want him to quit and start nagging, but she always said he'd be done with it when he got ready. She had work friends and a few associates from school. She didn't talk to Lori at all unless it was a casual conversation when they were all together. Baywood was more than okay with it.

"So you want to steam up my bedroom with your hell water shower?" Tina called as she walked through the door. Baywood smirked before pushing the clear shower curtain over a little as a silent invite. Since she slept naked, Tina stepped right in behind him. "Why you up so early?"

Baywood sighed, "I told you about G's twin right?" Tina nodded. "Well, he just got back from visiting Baby and apparently, Tameka set the whole thing up."

"Really? I'm not surprised," Tina said. "G did her pretty wrong."

Baywood nodded. "Any way it falls, Jean is out for blood. Don't know if Tameka knows since no one knows where she is, but if you happen to run into her...don't talk to her."

Tina frowned. "You know we were never like that anyway."

Baywood turned around and hugged her waist before kissing her. "I know." Tina wrapped her arms around his neck and smiled at him.

"Can I get some before you leave," she asked. Baywood laughed.

"You sound like a nigga."

"You know I don't like that word."

"Yeah yeah, I know," he said, pushing her up against the wall and lifting her left leg around his waist. "Get over it." Baywood licked just underneath Tina's chin as he moved with her against their shower wall. One of the most

40

satisfying things about being her husband was watching the serene look on her face that only he could get out of her. She looked so peaceful and if he could he'd stay like that for hours.

But business called for both of them.

After their shower, they both got dressed. Tina offered to make him breakfast, but he told her he'd grab something later. After kissing his wife goodbye, Baywood hit the block.

Riding around made him think of the times when him, Twan and Gino first started out on the block. A lot of things had changed. Baywood wasn't even sure what he was hustling for anymore. Something told him that his two best friends being six feet under should be his sign that it was time to hang it up. He just had no clue what else he would do.

Baywood parked in front of the cash house and called Chase.

"I'm already here, bro."

Baywood frowned. "Where's your car?"

"Lo got it."

"Aight."

Baywood parked behind the house and used his code to get into the back door. It was quiet, just how he liked it to be on count day. Chase was pulling duffle bags into the living room when he came in.

"Ain't no more?" he asked, only seeing four.

"No."

"What you mean?"

"What part you ain't understand?"

"The 'n'," Baywood said. They looked at each other and laughed.

"I put three up at the other spot, but this it."

Baywood sighed, sitting on the couch to open a bag. "Times are hard."

"That's why my pimp hand strong," Chase said. Baywood laughed.

"Yeah right, Lori would chop you up."

"Man, that's a evil little pregnant woman," Chase said.

"Stop knocking her up."

Chase smiled, "I'm done."

Baywood kept quiet as he opened his notebook, flipped to a new page and wrote the date at the top. It wasn't until they were done with one bag each that Chase said something else.

"So what you really think about this dude showing up?"

"I don't really feel no type of way about it," Baywood said. "We know we didn't pop Gino."

Chase chuckled. "You right."

"And I get him wanting to know what happened to his blood," Baywood said. "Wish I had more to give 'em. Gino was ruthless but he did right by me."

Chase nodded before running his right hand over his fade. "Got a feeling my shorty know more than she putting on though and I ain't really trying to beef with this cat over my fam. You know I'll go to war for them."

"Only thing she'd know is Tameka's whereabouts right?" Baywood said. "She needs to give her info up before he thinks she's hiding something else."

"She ain't even told me though, but I think Meka calls her every now and then to check on the kids. Shorty ain't gon rat her out."

"I heard Jean talking about offing whoever is really responsible. I don't know if dude about that life or not, but his twin was. We got other stuff to worry about so we need to just keep out of his personal business so he can keep it moving and we can get back to business."

Chase nodded. "I'll talk to her."

Jean sat parked in his rental on Main Street with a blunt in hand. It had been a few days since he'd been back from visiting Baby, but his next move had to be thought out carefully. He knew exactly what needed to be done to get her out of jail, however he didn't want it to ruin the rest of his plan.

Jean had memorized the address Gino had given him of Camryn's home. This was the first time he'd been there since being in town. He wasn't sure what he expected to find, but it was a little weird looking at it. Knowing what all had happened in that house and seeing it made him feel like he could relive those times through his brother's eyes.

He wondered what she named the baby. If he looked like they did when they were younger or if he took after his mom. Jean never even wanted kids so he figured a nephew was the next best thing.

Jean remembered Gino coming home one weekend, distraught and acting out of character. Their grandmother was sure it had something to do with Tameka, but once the two brothers had been out of range of her listening ear,

Gino confided in Jean about Camryn. At the time, he was under the assumption that Twan had terminated her pregnancy as instructed, and Jean could tell that Gino regretted it the moment he had given his best friend the order.

The pictures that Jean had seen of Camryn probably did her no justice. She wasn't Gino's usual type and that was probably why he fell in love with her so hard. Jean just wished his stubborn ways hadn't forced him into going down a path that he could have prevented. His brother could still be alive if he had followed his first mind to take Camryn away and start a new life with his family.

Jean soon became angry that Camryn hadn't tried to at least reach out to their grandmother. He knew that she'd been down for the funeral and found out Camryn was still pregnant with a little boy. Hadn't she known that they would want to know their family? That they had a right to?

Jean shook his head of those thoughts and began to focus on his next move. He had to validate Baby's story before he pulled his get-out-of-jail card for her and he knew there was only one person alive now who could do that.

Lori giggled as Chase playfully poked at her rounded belly while talking to the baby.

"Little dude, you better come out a boy," he said.

"That doesn't even make sense," Lori said, laughing.

"Not to you, this is man talk."

Lori laughed harder. "Okay, Chase."

The twins were at day care and Lori was grateful. She couldn't wait until they turned four to get some structure in their lives. She had to admit, she was very overwhelmed at times when they were first born, especially with Chase being in jail. She let them get away with a lot and by the time they were two, they were terrorizers. The only person who could really deal with them was Meka. When Chase got home, it took them a little while to listen to him, but now everything seemed to be calming down.

"They said it's a boy, but you never know so keep praying," Lori said, remembering how her doctor said her twins would be two girls.

"You just want it to be a girl because you got Jay so spoiled," Chase said. Lori smirked, but did not respond. He leaned over and kissed her belly before stretching and turning to get out of the bed.

"You leaving?"

"Yeah, gotta go handle some stuff."

Lori pouted. "Stay with me today."

"I stayed with you yesterday, big baby."

Lori huffed and Chase laughed at her.

"I'm bored with all y'all gone."

"Get a job then."

".....I'm good."

Chase laughed. "Come take a shower with me."

Smiling hard, Lori wiggled out of bed and followed her man into the bathroom. An hour later, when he finally got out the door, Lori decided to take a walk to the corner store. The weather was starting to turn a little, but it was still a nice day. She spoke to a few people on her way and a couple of teenagers who were skipping school stopped to feel her belly. She was almost to the store when a truck pulled on the side of her. She already knew who it was, but she kept walking.

"Why won't he just leave it alone," Lori mumbled to herself when she heard the truck's engine die and the door open.

"Good morning, Lori."

"....Good morning, Jean."

"Don't sound so happy to see me," he said, holding the door open to the store for her. Lori rolled her eyes, but thanked him anyway. She walked around the store, trying to make sure she had everything she was craving. Jean popped up on the other side of the ice cream freezer, running his hands down his fade.

"What you want?"

"I know you know where Meka is. I know you know she had something to do with my twin's death. It would be better for you and your family if you just told me what you know."

Lori looked at him for a moment and then smiled. "Listen, you seem to think you know a lot about a life Gino led that no one even knew you existed in. One thing he may not have told you was that him and I hated each other. He did Meka wrong on a daily and she sat back and allowed it. I, for one, told her to leave him alone, but no one listens to me."

"Your point?"

"My point is....get a life. Don't ask me shit else about what happened."

The more Jean looked at Lori, the more he understood why Gino never liked her. She was too cocky about her little cozy life. She didn't understand that Jean had more control over it than she thought.

"You have a good day," he said, walking past her. Lori stepped aside to make sure they didn't touch as he walked by. She waited until he was out of the store to suck her teeth.

"I'm going to kill Meka when I see her," she mumbled. "Still causing drama."

Jean watched from a distance as Lori hurried down the street as best as she could with her belly. He shook his head, realizing that she wasn't going to give up Tameka's whereabouts so easy.

He waited until she was walking up the walkway to her door before jumping out of his truck. Lori turned around quickly when she heard his truck.

"What are you doing?" she yelled. He quickly pulled her around to the side of the house and out of clear sight. Her eyes widened as he pushed her up against the wall by her neck.

"You seem to think I'm playing with you," Jean said. "I was trying to be nice, but you really don't have too many options. This won't go how you think it will."

"Chase is going to kill you," Lori mumbled, trying to move his hand. "Wait until I tell him."

"You think I'm scared?" he laughed and leaned closer to her. "I'm more like my twin than you think Lori. Don't cross me."

Lori swallowed and remained quiet. The look in his eyes was all too familiar. It sent chills down her back just like Gino used to.

"I don't know where she is," she admitted. "She only calls me from private numbers."

He looked at her for a moment, trying to figure out if she was lying. Lori sighed when he let her go, but didn't move out of her space.

"I'm gonna get what I came here for and I'll go through anybody I have to for it to happen," he said. "If she calls you, find out something useful."

Lori frowned, but nodded slowly. She didn't move until she heard him get back into his truck.

Jean sighed, running his hands down his face before he put the truck in drive and reached for the blunt in the ashtray. He wasn't like his twin, he wouldn't put his hands on a woman, especially not a pregnant one, but Lori seemed to get under his skin.

He had to control himself for his plan to work, which means he needed someone else to make sure everything went smoothly. Jean knew who to call to help him out.

Jean pulled out his cell phone and called Remy.

"Yo!" she answered.

"Feel like taking a trip?"

Not even two days later, Jean was sitting in the parking lot of the Amtrak station, waiting for Remy. She was catching the bus and was due to arrive at any minute. Jean had to admit that he was a little excited for Remy to be coming. It helped to know he had someone around that he could trust.

Remy always reminded Jean of the actress Reagan Gomez from the old Parent 'Hood, only Remy was taller and thinner with dark red hair. She always kept her look real simple and classy, but her mouth and attitude was far from it. Jean used to worry about her getting her heart broken all the time when they were in high school. Gino used to say that Remy could handle herself. Jean didn't believe him until he saw Remy actually beat up one of her ex-boyfriends and get suspended from school.

Remy didn't like that Gino had moved away from home and gotten so involved in the drug game, especially with Jean being sick all the time and their grandmother getting older. She felt he needed to be around family more and ultimately, she was right.

"Hello brother," Remy greeted Jean as she always did once she got in the car. He nodded and began to pull out of the parking lot. "I don't suppose you want to feed me right now do you?"

"We can get some food after you get settled in the room."

"I'm not staying in yours?"

"Got one next door."

"Cool...cause you snore."

Jean laughed before lightly pushing the side of her head. Remy smiled and punched his leg.

"Quit acting, you know you want to sleep with me."

Remy frowned as if a stench filled the air and burned her nose. Jean laughed hard and eventually Remy did too. "You play too much."

"I missed you, sis."

"Yeah…you only miss me when you need something."

Jean sobered up. "I'm tired of playing with this chick."

Remy held her hand up. "Explain after you feed me."

Jean nodded and went in the direction of the nearest Denny's, it was Remy's favorite and he needed to butter her up to get his plan to work.

Jean opted for a steak omelette while Remy had half the breakfast menu spread out in front of her.

"When's the last time you ate?" he asked.

Remy looked up at him from her plate and bit her lip. "…Not that long ago."

Jean watched her for a moment, looking for signs of malnourishment. Remy could tell what he was doing, so she cleared her throat and took a sip of her orange juice.

"Remy."

"I've been eating," she snapped. "Tell me what you sent me down here for."

Jean sighed before sitting up. "Her name is Lori. She knows where Meka is."

"You know this for sure?"

"She been acting tight since I popped up, saying little stuff. Even questioned me about whose name the house was in."

Remy nodded in understanding. "And we're sure Meka's hiding something?"

Jean sucked his teeth. "What you think I'm doing down here?"

"What did Tati say when you went to visit her?" Remy asked, ignoring his attitude. Jean couldn't do anything but laugh. When he first presented her with all the information, Remy refused to call Tati by her nickname. Said one grown woman shouldn't be calling another grown woman Baby. "Did she say Meka actually pulled the trigger?"

"Nah, but she set my brother up," Jean said, feeling his blood boil again. "All because she couldn't handle a side chick."

Remy laughed. "I never liked her."

"You didn't know her," Jean said matter-of-factly.

"I knew enough. Why don't you let me handle her?"

"Already promised her to Baby."

"How we know she's telling the truth. She could be just trying to get out of jail."

"She has no way of knowing if I can get her out or not and I'm not relying on just what she says," Jean said, looking out of the window of the Denny's to a town he hated. He knew this town sucked his brother into a world he wouldn't have known if he would have just stayed home. Jean knew that his twin wasn't a saint by any means, but whatever he did wasn't worth his life. He planned to make whoever was responsible pay. "I know something's not right."

Remy continued to eat. If Jean hadn't known her as well as he did, he would have thought that Remy wasn't listening. Once she was done with her bowl of grits she sat back and looked at him while finishing her juice.

"So Lori's pregnant...I can't do much."

Jean nodded, deciding not to tell her about their little confrontation.

"Why she even defending a chick who left her anyway?"

"That's what I need to find out."

"And that's why I'm here."

"Her dude ain't sitting well with me either, but I don't need any drama with them disrupting my mission. All they gotta do is give up Meka's whereabouts and we gone."

Remy nodded. "What about the baby momma?"

Jean sighed as his fist tightened and released under the table. "I got that under control."

FIVE

"I don't think we should do so much for his first birthday. I'm already broke since Christmas is next week."

"No one told you to buy all those toys he's not going to play with," Nana said.

Camryn sucked her teeth. "Most of them are learning activity toys. He's going to be a baby genius." Camryn beamed down at Ian as he clapped along with Mickey Mouse on the television.

Nana laughed. "Okay, Cam."

Camryn had to laugh at herself as she switched her phone to her other ear. Christmas was a few days away and Ian would be one at the end of next month on his father's birthday.

This week was the first anniversary of his death.

All week, her stomach has been in knots. Every time she went to sleep, she relived their last time together. Camryn had to stop herself from crying in front of Ian because he looked so much like him. She had to admit that she thought her life would be easier away from Gino and everything that happened, but it only seemed more torturous. Trying to convince Nana and Mia that she was okay, raising Ian on her own; it was all overwhelming her.

"Camryn."

"Yes ma'am."

"I'll call you back after my doctor's appointment."

Camryn immediately switched into concerned granddaughter mode. "Are you okay?" Camry constantly worried about Nana, especially since they did not live together anymore. Lupus had no cure.

"I'm fine, just a check up," she said quickly, which let Camryn know that she was lying. Deciding not to push the issue, Camryn accepted her answer and ended the call.

She sat back on the couch and idly watched Mickey Mouse with Ian, trying to get her mind together. She had already requested the next few days off of work, knowing she would be no good there, but now she wished she had taken the overtime.

She wanted to call Mia, but she figured she would be tied up with Jeremiah. After a few minutes, she called anyway.

"Hey boo," Mia asked. Camryn smiled at her excitement.

"Hey best friend, I'm bored."

Mia laughed. "Me too and I just got home from work. You didn't go today?"

"No, took a few days off," Camryn said, opting not to mention why.

"Well, good. You need a break."

"To do what though?" Camryn asked. Mia giggled.

"We could make Jeremiah watch Ian and go get pedicures."

"I can't ask him to do that again," Camryn said, already feeling bad for having Jeremiah watch him the few times he did.

"Girl bye, what would I have a wonderful boyfriend for if he can't watch my godson for a few hours!"

Camryn laughed. "Ian does like him."

"Ian loves him."

"Aw!" Cam teased. Mia laughed. "He's at work?"

"No, he's been sleeping since I got off work. Once he gets up and I feed him, I'll let you know when."

"Are you shacking up, Miss Mia?" Camryn teased.

Mia sucked her teeth. "You know better. He only has a little while longer to get my ring before I drop him."

"You're so lying."

".....Bye!"

Camryn laughed when Mia hung up on her. She was so grateful for her best friend. Mia seemed to be her only friend.

Camryn ended up giving Ian a bath so that he'd be ready for his afternoon nap and wouldn't bother Jeremiah too much. She was exited and way over due for a pedicure. Plus, she kind of wanted to talk with Mia about what she had been feeling lately.

Mia called about twenty minutes later telling Cam to come over. They had been staying in the apartment buildings opposite each other ever since Cam moved up that way before Ian was born. Jayson had stayed in the same apartment complex as Cam until he moved away.

"What's up, little man?" Jeremiah asked, taking Ian from Cam. Ian looked at him for a second before his lips curved into a smile and he began to laugh.

"You sure you don't mind watching him?" Cam asked, putting Ian's diaper bag down next to the couch. Jeremiah waved her off.

"Y'all go on and have girl time," Jeremiah said, walking over and sitting on the floor with Ian. He began pulling random toys out and imitating their sounds, which made Ian laugh harder. Camryn laughed as well, happy to see that her son was excited to play with Jeremiah. It made leaving Ian with him a little easier.

"Bye baby," Mia said, leaning down to meet Jeremiah's lips for a goodbye kiss. "Come on girl."

"We won't be gone long," Cam said as Mia pulled her out of the door. She pouted when she got in the car.

"What?"

"He didn't even notice I was gone," she said. Mia frowned at her before laughing. "What?"

"You mad because he's not as attached to you as he used to be?"

"He's not even one yet and he almost doesn't need me anymore."

Mia laughed harder before patting her friend's knee. "Geez, I hope I'm not as bad as you are when I'm a mom."

Cam sucked her teeth. "Hell, you'll be worse."

They laughed in agreement as Mia drove off towards the shopping plaza where their favorite nail shop was. There was a little wait but nothing too heavy.

Cam sighed as the hot water relaxed her flat feet and she pushed her back into the massage chair. This would definitely help her relieve some of her anxiety. She was zoned out until she heard Mia tell the owner that she was footing the bill for both of them.

"Why you paying for me?"

"…Because I know what this week is."

Cam looked at Mia to gauge her facial expressions. The solemn look that Mia gave her, allowed Cam to know that Mia truly did know what this week was.

"Mia, I'm fine."

"I know," Mia said quickly. "I just wanted to get you out the house and get your mind off of it for a little while."

Instead of denying it, Cam nodded and tried to continue to relax.

"Thanks."

"…So, how you feel about it?"

"I'm sorry love, I don't really want to talk about it," Cam admitted. "Been trying hard not to think about it but looking at Ian…"

"He looks a lot like him," Mia said, finishing Cam's thought. She nodded "He's so much more handsome though right?"

Cam laughed. "I won't deny that," she said, thinking of her son's smiling face.

"I know you don't want to talk about it, but I am worried about you," Mia confessed. "You haven't really made any friends."

"You don't have friends," Cam defended.

"I have a few associates outside of you and Jeremiah. Camryn, you don't talk to anyone else."

She sighed. Cam almost wanted to take her feet out of the water and walk home. She was tired of hearing the same thing from Mia and Nana, even Jayson used to say she needed more friends. To Camryn, friends were overrated. She had done pretty well in life with just Mia and Nana and now that she was raising Ian, she really didn't have time for friends.

What Camryn wanted was a love to replace the one that wouldn't leave her heart, even if she wanted it to.

"So you and Jeremiah seem to be getting real serious," Cam said, changing the subject. Although Mia knew exactly what she was doing, she let her anyway.

"I know right," Mia said, blushing. "I was scared to go there with him at first but he's like a dream. I keep waiting for the other shoe to drop."

Cam sighed. "Mia, don't think like that. Jeremiah's one of the good guys. You got blessed....well, he really got the bigger blessing."

Mia giggled. "Stop gassing me."

"I never had to do that," Cam said, honestly. "I wouldn't have gotten through my pregnancy had it not been for you and Nana."

"What about Jayson?"

Cam side-eyed her and Mia threw her hands up in surrender. Cam knew that Mia wasn't happy about Cam deciding not to try a long distance relationship with Jayson. She respected her opinion but with her being her best friend and Jayson's cousin, she wanted Mia to stay out of it.

After their pedicures, they stopped and picked up enough food for Jeremiah and Ian at Popeye's and headed back to Mia's.

"Just in time," Jeremiah said. "We're hungry!"

Ian made noises as if he was saying he was hungry as well. He wasn't making coherent words yet, but he said a lot to only be 11 months. Mia laughed at them as they all sat down in the living room to eat.

Cam watched how Mia and Jeremiah acted towards each other and it warmed her heart with different emotions. They moved so naturally with each other. She knew that Jeremiah truly loved her best friend and wouldn't be shocked if they got married soon. She was beyond elated for Mia. She was never really a dater in school because she focused so much on her education. Mia would be graduating with her Bachelor's within the year and she deserved to be happy.

On the other hand, Cam's heart hurt. Didn't she deserve to be happy, too?

After Cam and Ian left Mia's place, she headed home to get him ready for bed. He was still a little wound up from playing with Jeremiah, so she let him play with a few toys and watch his favorite show for a little while to get him sleepy. While straightening up his room, Cam thought about what Mia said. A few of her co-workers at the store she worked at always tried to get her to go out with them after work and she constantly turned them down.

Ever since Meka gave her that $250,000, she went to working part-time. She still didn't have an immediate plan on her future and she would need to pick a major at school soon. That money wouldn't last her a lifetime, so she needed a plan.

Feeling a little motivated after Ian went to sleep, Cam sat down on the couch with her legs folded under her and a pillow on her lap to keep her laptop from heating up her thighs. She knew she loved psychology, but she never thought about how that would translate into a career.

She started with a search on jobs in psychology and went from there. After going through a few of them, Cam narrowed it down between a sports psychologist and a school psychologist.

"Let's see what Nana thinks," she said to herself. While she was reaching for her cell phone, Jayson called. To even her surprise, she answered.

"What you up to?" he asked. "I know little man is sleep."

"He is," she said. "Looking at some psychology careers I'm interested in."

"Really? That's good."

"Yeah, time for me to make a decision about my future."

Jayson snickered. "You're only 21 love, you have some time."

"I have a son," Cam said, matter-of-factly. "Time isn't on my side."

"...I'm coming home to visit soon."

Cam sighed, already knowing. "Yes, Mia said your mom has been hounding you."

"I haven't even been gone that long," he joked. Cam didn't laugh. Long enough in her opinion. "Can I see you and Ian when I visit?"

"...We'll see."

"I can live with that."

"You sure can," she mumbled. Cam sighed, trying to will herself to stop being so mean to Jayson for following his dream career. "What you up to? Your show is about to come on."

Jayson laughed. "I have it set to record so I can skip past the commercials. Plus, I missed your voice."

"It is pretty nice, huh?" Cam teased. Jayson laughed and she couldn't help but smile.

"I'm hoping we can at least get back to being friends, like we were in the beginning," he admitted.

"You mean when you were judging me for being pregnant by a drug dealer?" she asked, a hint of amusement in her voice.

"Not that beginning, more of when you started helping me with demographics for work."

Cam laughed. "That sounds like a plan."

SIX

Remy wiggled her toes as she lounged on Jean's hotel room bed, waiting for him to get dressed. She had been in town for two days and hadn't done much of anything. She was able to at least meet a few people, including Lori, but Jean told her to hold off on anything until he gave his signal. Remy was impatient, but she'd play by her godbrother's rules this time. Finding out what happened and finding her little nephew was important enough for her to actually listen to someone else.

Thinking about her godbrother that was no longer breathing made her stomach turn. She was never good with relationships and Gino and Jean had gotten her out of a lot of dumb situations throughout her life. They truly were her brothers and Remy would do anything she could to honor that.

"About time," she said when Jean came out of the bathroom, clasping his watch around his wrist.

"If you would have stayed in your room until I was done you wouldn't be sitting looking silly."

Remy sucked her teeth and stood from the bed. "Let's go."

Jean looked at her and laughed before grabbing his wallet and keys. Baywood and Chase were throwing a BBQ up the block for Christmas. That was the good thing about living in the South, you didn't have to worry about winter ruining any outdoor plans most of the time.

"So we'll make it back home before Thursday right?" Remy asked, knowing that if they didn't spend Christmas with her mom and Granny Watson, they'd never hear the end of it.

"Yeah, we'll head up there that morning. Hopefully, you can stay home."

Remy nodded, knowing that meant she had two days to get what she needed out of Lori for that plan to work.

The BBQ was at Herman Park. It wasn't a very big park but the way everyone in town was up there you would think it was. Jean parked near the main entrance and sat listening to the radio while waiting for Remy to finish smoking her blunt. He looked over her outfit and shook his head. He always had an attitude about her showing so much, but since she was grown now, he kept his mouth closed. However, he wanted to make sure she was focused on what she was there for.

"Remy," he said.

"Huh?"

"Don't start nothing up here."

Remy's eyes lit up in amusement and she laughed. "What you mean?"

"You know what I mean," he said, wondering why she thought he was joking.

"I can't look? Dang!"

"We got business here, I don't need to be worried about you and these dudes."

Remy sighed and sucked her teeth. "You never let me have any fun."

Jean didn't respond, only waited for her to finish. Once she was done, they headed into the park.

Jean and Remy ran into Baywood first. He was walking away from the swing set with a little boy next to him. It was Jacob, Lori and Chase's son.

"About time y'all made it up here," he said, greeting Jean with a handshake and Remy with a hug.

"You practicing?" Jean joked, referring to Jacob. Baywood frowned and shook his head hard. Remy and Jean laughed.

"We don't have time for kids," Baywood said. "I'll let Chase and Lo have that...Come on, we over here."

They walked with Baywood over to the largest gondola where everyone was. The smell of BBQ was in the air and there were bottles of alcohol lined up on one picnic table. Coolers with juice, soda and water sat under them.

"This was nice of y'all," Remy said. Baywood nodded.

"Yeah, we didn't always do this type of stuff," he said. Jean knew that meant they didn't do it when Gino was in charge. Jean sat at the end of the picnic table Baywood and his people were at with his back up against the table and his legs out the opposite way so he could see everyone. Remy sat with her back up against him and her legs on either side of the bench.

"Y'all playing Spades?" she asked Lori. She nodded.

"Can you play?" Chase asked. "Cause she can't."

"Shut up, jerk!" Lori said, frowning. Chase blew her a kiss from across the table.

"Here," Remy said, leaning over. "I'll help you."

"Help her cheat?" Moe, one of Baywood's dealers asked.

"Shut up, you was losing anyway even with her being horrible," Tina said. They all laughed.

Jean kept an eye on Remy, wondering what angle she was working with Lori. Remy could be a loose cannon, but he hoped he had made her realize how little time they had to get what they needed. His plan was to lay low a little while after they found out where Tameka was. He'd keep some tabs on her until he could get Baby out of jail and hold up his end of the deal. Until then, he had to deal with Camryn and the baby.

"When you due again?" Remy asked.

"Three more months," Chase said, proudly. Remy watched Lori glance from Moe to Chase and smile.

"He's counting better than I am," she joked. Remy smirked as she put down the Ace of Diamonds and kept her eye on Moe.

"I haven't met you yet," she said, licking her lips. "You're cute. I might let you take me out tonight."

Moe looked at her and laughed, licking his own lips. "That right?"

"Yeah, give me your number."

"What are you doing?" Jean whispered in her ear. She turned to him and smiled.

"Watch me work, bro."

Jean huffed in irritation before a young lady brought him a drink. "What's in this?"

"Ciroc and Sprite."

He nodded and thanked her before asking for a beer. Remy turned and eyed him.

"Calm down, I got this."

He looked at her for a minute before nodding.

Jean looked around at everything and let Remy handle her end. He noticed now that he had been in town for a couple of weeks that people were really warming up to him. The same girl who bought him a drink, fixed his plate and made sure he had whatever he needed. People started asking him about Gino as a kid. That made him smile.

"Was he always an OG?" someone asked. Jean laughed, adjusting his shades.

"I remember when we were in high school, Remy had two dudes fighting to take her to prom," he said.

Remy sucked her teeth. "Here you go!"

"What happened?" Moe asked.

"We were chilling at lunch and Remy sitting watching these dudes box like it was fight night. One of them started talking crazy to Rem and I immediately wanted to shut it down. G sat there for a minute not saying anything. Pissed me off. All the sudden, one of the dudes grabs at Remy to yank her off her chair."

"Next thing we know, G is bashing dude's head in with the lunch tray," Remy cut in, laughing. "I start kicking him and Jean sitting there telling people to back up and make sure the guards wasn't coming."

"So he wasn't a punk," Lori mumbled. Remy eyed her.

"Far from it."

Chase cleared his throat. "G didn't really get his hands dirty around here, but we could tell he was a beast."

"That he was," Jean mumbled. "No doubt about that."

A little girl came up behind Chase and Jean recognized her to be the girl twin, Tia.

"Daddy, play with me!"

"Give me a minute, T," Chase said. He looked at Baywood and nodded. Baywood finished his drink before going to sit next to Jean. Chase sat on the other side.

"What's up?" Jean asked.

"You still been staying in that hotel?" Baywood asked.

Jean frowned. "Yeah, why?"

"If you thinking of staying, we got a place we can put you up in," Chase said. Jean looked at him for a moment.

"If I was thinking of staying, I would just stay in my brother's house."

Baywood nodded. "Right."

"Why would I be thinking of staying?"

"Look," Baywood said. "I feel like I owe G a lot. He put me on and although we built this together, it wouldn't have been all this without him."

"So you trying to settle with me?" Jean asked.

"We can give you a block or two until you feel comfortable. See how it works out for you," Chase said. "You his twin, but ya'll ain't the same person. Feel me?"

Jean laughed. "Yeah, we not."

"You need some time to think about it?" Baywood asked.

"Nah. Thanks for the offer, but I'm good."

"You got a job or something?" Chase asked. "You been here a long time. How you living?"

"I'm living," Jean said, looking at him. "That's all you need to know."

Chase's nose flared a little and Jean could feel himself get a little anxious at the thought of being able to physically harm him. He hadn't had a fight in a while and although he controlled his anger well, he would definitely have fun.

Baywood, seeing that the situation was getting tense, threw his hands up to diffuse it. "Look, we just wanted to look out for you if you needed work."

Jean nodded, showing his respect for Baywood by cooling down. "Thanks, but no thanks."

It was after dark when everyone left the park and Remy and Jean headed back to the hotel. Jean had some questions for Remy, but he could tell that she was drunk. She got ignorant when she was and Jean didn't feel like arguing with her, so he decided to save that for in the morning.

He got her in her room safely and headed to his. He had an alert on his email that he had been itching to check but didn't want to do it at the park with so many eyes around.

Jean smiled as he opened the email that contained just the information he needed. It was the address to Camryn's apartment. It had taken him a while to convince his connect in the state's office to give it up, but when he made him an offer he couldn't refuse, he'd sent it right away.

His plan was picking up momentum. After a small Christmas break at home with Granny Watson, Jean would be paying Camryn and the baby a visit.

Remy finger combed her hair in the mirror as she held her laugh in at the look Jean was giving her through the mirror.

"I thought I told you no boys."

"I thought I told you that I got this," she snapped. "Have a little faith, brother. I got this."

"What are you doing going on this date then?"

Remy sucked her teeth before turning to face him. "Will you let me do this, please?"

They had a stare down for a few minutes before Jean huffed and walked out of the bathroom. Remy smiled victoriously and then went back to getting ready. Moe would be there any minute. Jean stayed around her room to see if she would actually leave, when she came back into the room and grabbed her purse, he frowned.

"He not coming to the door?"

"He's in the lobby. He don't need this room number," Remy said. "Go do something."

Jean sighed when the door slammed.

Remy saw Moe standing near the entrance and sighed, making sure she played this date the right way. She had a hunch earlier at the park and usually her gut was never wrong. All she needed him to do was say the right thing and she'd have all the ammo needed.

"Hey Moe," she said hugging him and kissing the corner of his mouth. He licked his lips and held the door open for her. "Thank you."

"You not gon ask where we going?" he joked, walking towards his car.

"I ain't from here remember? Don't matter to me."

Moe laughed before they got in the car. Remy tried to look around his car without being noticeable, but it was clear that he cleaned it often.

"How old are you?" she asked.

"25."

"Um," she said. Moe laughed.

"What was that for?"

"Thought you were older."

"How old are you?"

"23, but you'll do for tonight."

Moe laughed harder. "You something else."

"That's what they tell me," she said, smiling and poking him in his right dimple. "You have a cute smile."

"Thugs ain't cute."

It was Remy's turn to laugh.

They rode for a little while until coming to a bar and grill that Remy had never heard of.

"I hope you can hold your liquor."

Moe smiled. "Sounds like a challenge. What you drinking?"

"Let's do fireball shots!" Remy said, clapping her hands and wiggling in her seat. The bartender eyed her before smirking at Moe.

"You met your match?" she asked. Moe laughed.

"We about to see."

They had four rounds of shots before finally ordering food and going to a booth in the corner. Remy couldn't tell if he was feeling the shots or not, but she knew she was, so she made a mental note to slow down.

Moe wasn't Remy's usual type, which made her mission a lot easier. He was shorter than most of the men she dated, but still had a few inches on her. His skin was dark and smooth other than few scars. His hair was faded on both sides with a low cut on top. She did like the fact that he had a gold grill in his mouth.

"I like how you made me take you out," he said, licking his lips.

"Oh, so you didn't want to?" she asked. Moe smiled.

"I didn't say all that."

"Well, it sounded like that so you owe me two shots."

Moe laughed and the waitress came back over and he ordered two more rounds of shots. They joked around and had a nice time. When Moe leaned back and ran his hand over his face, Remy knew he was drunk. She got up and slid close to him in the booth.

"I like you, Moe."

"I like you, too, Remy."

"You like me enough to help me out?" she asked. He leaned closer to her as she fingered his small beard.

"Help you out with what?"

"I need to find Meka," she said, pouting. "Gino and Jean are the only family I really got and Meka knows more than she told y'all."

"Man…"

Remy scooted closer and kissed his neck. "You would want to know what happened to your fam right?"

"Meka ain't never did nothing wrong to me to give her up, besides I really don't know, cutie."

"What about Chase?"

Moe eyes widened. "…What about him?"

Remy licked her lips and smiled evilly as she looked into his eyes. "He ever did you wrong?"

Moe cleared his throat and shook his head. "Nah, he's a cool boss, or whatever."

"So why you sexing his chick?"

Moe's breathing increased and his eye lids lowered. He leaned closer to Remy and whispered "Who told you that?"

Remy shrugged. "I've very observant….that your baby?"

Moe ran his hand down his face again. "Nah, but the one she lost was…I ain't touched her since, I swear. You can't tell nobody."

"Tell me what I need to know then."

Moe sighed. "I really don't know where Meka is, but I know for a fact that Lori does."

Remy nodded, knowing that much already.

"We good?" he asked.

Remy smiled. "As long as your girl tells me what I need to know, we're great."

Mia smiled in satisfaction at her reflection in the mirror, wanting to make sure everything was in place. Tonight was date night and seeing as she and Jeremiah hadn't had much alone time the last few weeks, she was excited. Their schedules usually didn't conflict as much, but since he had been working overtime, Mia rarely got to see her man.

She was looking forward to tonight.

Using his key, Jeremiah came into the apartment around 7. Mia knew he'd be on time, so she was ready to go.

"You actually dressed?" he asked, hugging her. She giggled before looking up to kiss him.

"I thought I'd surprise you tonight," she joked. Jeremiah grabbed her hand and made her slowly spin around.

"Nothing surprising about how good you look," he said. "Let's get this night started."

Mia smiled and grabbed her purse off the coffee table before she followed behind him out of the door.

Jeremiah was listening to an oldie station when they got in the car. Mia smiled, loving that they had similar tastes in music. In fact, the only thing they really disagreed on was football. Jeremiah was a Steelers fan and Mia loved the Cowboys.

Love Ballad by L.T.D came on and Jeremiah sang it loud and off key while rubbing Mia's hand.

"Sing baby," she said, laughing. Jeremiah eyed her and she covered her mouth.

"You trying to gas me," he said. Mia looked at him and shook her head while grinning. "It's okay, I appreciate it."

She laughed. "Get me to this restaurant you keep talking about. I'm hungry."

Jeremiah looked at her briefly and smiled a smile that made her heart stop. "I got you, baby."

Every day, it became harder and harder for Mia to remain a virgin. She almost couldn't believe that they'd made it a year. Jeremiah was patient and although they had a few close calls, they kept their commitment to God.

Mia wanted to cry just thinking about it. She used to think that maybe he was getting it from somewhere else. However, the more she got to know him, the more she trusted that he was in their relationship for real. They were dating with intent and Mia was elated about it.

Jeremiah took Mia to Copia. It was a nice restaurant that was famous for their wine. Mia tried not to indulge much because it made her very affectionate. She giggled and told herself to behave as Jeremiah came around and opened her door. They walked hand in hand into the restaurant and since Jeremiah had a reservation, they were seated right away.

"Hope you got big pockets tonight, I'm hungry," she teased.

"When are you not?"

They both laughed before Mia hit him in his arm. "Shut it up."

"You know I love you, big hungry."

"You need to quit!" Mia said, laughing.

After they ordered, they filled each other in on the other's day. Jeremiah ran a small car detailing business and he also bought homes that had been foreclosed on, fixed them up and rented them out. He had been looking at properties all day that his partner said was a good investment.

"You didn't like any of them?" Mia asked.

"Babe, all of them were trash."

"Well, you supposed to fix them up."

"Them houses needed Jesus."

Mia laughed before shaking her head. "I'm sure they weren't that bad."

Jeremiah frowned before pulling his phone out and showing her a couple of pictures. "I don't know what Kenny was thinking."

"You right," Mia said, shaking her head at the pictures. "You should have taken some Holy oil with you."

They both laughed. The waitress came out with two glasses of wine.

"When you order that?" Mia asked.

"While you were in the bathroom," he said, wrapping both of his hands around each glass and the waitress walked off.

"I don't need any, baby," Mia said. Jeremiah grinned before holding the one out in his left hand.

"You'll love this, just taste it."

Mia sighed before taking the glass, she was about to sip it but as soon as she raised it to her lips, she felt something clink against the glass. With it still to her lips, Mia looked down into the wine and her heart stopped.

"What is this?" Mia asked, still holding the wine glass in place, but looking at Jeremiah.

"What does it look like?"

"Jeremiah," Mia warned. "Don't play with me."

"Oh, I'm sure that ring shows that I'm definitely not playing with you."

Mia's eyes watered as she put the glass down and quickly fished the ring out and thrust it into Jeremiah's face. He chuckled before wiping it off with his napkin and holding Mia's left hand from across the small table.

"When we got together, I told you I was dating for a purpose. It didn't take me long to figure out that you were it. Plain and simple. No long, drawn-out speech. I'm ready to build a real life with you as my wife. Will you marry me?"

"Definitely!" she said, squealing.

He laughed. "Can't be regular, huh?" Jeremiah put the ring on my finger. Mia held her hand out before standing up and sitting in his lap.

"My non-regular-ness is why you love me," she said, wrapping her arms around his neck. Jeremiah rubbed her chin as they kissed.

"Can you believe it. He actually proposed to me!" Mia squealed into the phone. Cam tried to act surprised. She was with Jeremiah when he purchased the ring.

"I can believe it," Cam said. "You didn't expect it?"

"Maybe not this soon, I don't know," Mia said. "I'm just so excited right now. I'm getting married."

"Yes, you are!"

"I need to set a date…"

"Slow down girl," Cam said. "Enjoy being engaged."

"You're right. I gotta call Jayson and Auntie."

"You didn't tell them yet?"

"No, I called you right after I called Momma."

"Aren't you still on a date? Where is Jeremiah."

"Girl, he's sleep!" Mia said. Cam giggled. "I can't even think of sleep right now."

"Well, I'm about to get in the shower so call your family and I'll talk to you in the morning."

Cam sighed, the guilt of her feelings sitting on her like weights. She had known for a few weeks that Jeremiah was proposing to Mia, but now that he'd done it, she felt weird about it.

It was one thing when they were dating, but Mia was all Cam had besides Ian, with Nana being out of state. Would them getting married cause Mia not to be there for Cam like she had been?

They had only been dating a year. Cam thought it seemed a little pretentious for Jeremiah to propose so soon. Yes, Mia was a great woman, but was she ready for marriage? Jeremiah was technically her first real boyfriend and Mia was a few months shy of 22. It wouldn't hurt for them to wait a couple of years.

Cam checked in on Ian to make sure he was still asleep before heading to bed herself. She debated on if she wanted to take her sleeping pills or not. Lately, she had been having nightmares about what happened last year. She figured since the anniversary of it was passing, they would go away. Christmas was in two days and she had a lot to do. Not getting any sleep wasn't really an option.

Before she could get comfortable, Nana called.

"What are you doing up?" Cam asked. "Everything okay?"

"No, Mia just sent me something but I can't open it."

Cam laughed. "It was probably a picture of her engagement ring."

"Engagement ring! Well, alright!"

Cam giggled at her grandmother's reaction. "You don't think it's too early."

"Well, that's not for us to decide, but I was 20 when I married your grandfather."

Cam nodded, remembering the story.

"It was different in those days though, Nana."

"Watch it," she said. "What's the real issue?"

"…I just don't want her moving too fast." Nana laughed. "What?"

"I can recall a certain granddaughter of mine telling her best friend to mind her own business when she was giving advice about the father of your child."

Cam bit her lip.

"Yeah, but that was different."

"How is it different? You thought you were in love right? That he was the one?" Cam got quiet. "Let that girl live. Jeremiah is a great young man and if he wants to marry your best friend, you should be just as happy as I'm sure she is."

"I am happy for her," Cam mumbled.

"You don't sound like it."

Cam sighed. "I guess I'm just cranky," she lied.

"About what?"

"I been having dreams about Tameka and Gino."

"That sounds like a nightmare."

"It doesn't start off that way. I can't even really explain it, but it feels like those visions I had of Momma when I first got pregnant," Cam admitted.

"Mmph…"

"What?"

"I'll have to look in my dream book."

Cam sucked her teeth. "Really, Nana?"

"I'm serious. It has to mean something if you keep dreaming about the past. It usually means it's coming back into your present."

"He's dead though…" Cam whispered.

"It may mean someone from the past or maybe that Ian has some of his qualities."

"Oh God, no!" Cam said, her heart pounding.

"He had some good ones, right?"

"Nana, you're being nice," Cam said. "But he did. When we were in love, he was very caring and funny and he always motivated me to study."

"Whatsoever things are true and good, think on these things," Nana said, paraphrasing the scripture.

Cam smiled. "You're right."

"Don't focus on the past," Nana said. "You have enough unexpected twists and turns in the future to think about."

Jean laughed hard as Remy pranced around his hotel room, telling him about her date with Moe.

"He looked like a deer in headlights when I bust him out!" she laughed. "I mean, I just had a hunch I didn't think dude would say he got her pregnant!"

"How'd you figure it out?"

"At the park when I asked Lori about the baby, she kept eyeing him and then when I started flirting with him she was fidgeting like she was irritated. Shit was obvious to me. I'm surprised her dude didn't catch it."

"Too busy worried about me," Jean mumbled. "So what's your next move?"

"I'll go see her in the morning, get what we need and we can head home for Christmas."

"Just like that huh?" Jean asked with a smirk.

"Just like that!" she said, giving him a high five. "I'm sure little miss white girl won't want her man knowing he was about to take care of somebody else baby."

Jean laughed. "She's mixed."

Remy sucked her teeth. "Whatever, Gino."

"Watch it," he said, eyeing her. Remy looked at him and raised her eyebrow.

"What? Nobody in here but us. I just can't call you Jean, it's weird."

"Well, don't say my name at all," Gino said. "Don't want my cover blown."

Remy sighed and nodded, finally sitting on the bed.

"You answer to his name good when they say it," she admitted.

"It was hard at first, but I know nobody knew him so when I hear it, I automatically know they talking to me."

"How long you think you gotta act like Jean?"

"Not too much longer," Gino said, rubbing his chin and leaning back on the headboard. "It's just about time for the big reveal."

SEVEN

"Bro, let me go back....I got this!"

Every morning when he woke up, Gino thought about how he'd be dead right now. So much had gone on since that night that he often thought it was all some type of nightmare. He thought he'd wake up, drive home, and kid around with his twin brother before heading back to the life he built as Gino, the drug lord.

That night last December, he had been ready to give it all up. He had been ready to mend fences with Camryn, divorce Tameka, and start over with his rightful family. A nagging feeling in his gut told him he'd been too late. He hadn't figured out that Twan was the snake, but he knew it would catch up to him soon and that was the only reason he'd gone home that night after meeting Camryn. He didn't want Granny Watson and Jean to be surprised or lost if something went down.

Jean had persuaded him to let him go back in his place. Gino laughed at him, but Jean was persistent. Told him that he wasn't thinking clear, especially not after spending time with Camryn and he'd handle it all. Jean never took an interest in Gino's life or any life outside of the house for that matter. Gino told him that he was crazy; that he didn't have it in him.

Jean told him he'd prove it.

Gino regretted his decision to give in everyday since Granny Watson got the call that two people at a house that was in her name were dead. He done a lot of wrong in his life and there were only a few things he regretted. He hadn't really dealt with having to add his twin's death to that list.

His sadness completely switched to anger when he thought of his wife. He had to admit that he didn't think Tameka had it in her to put a plan together, but she had. For the life of him, Gino couldn't figure out why she just didn't leave. All he put her through and she stayed without question. He must have drove her crazy, because thinking she would get away with setting him up for the kill was insane. He was sure that Lori had contacted her about "Gino's twin" already. Gino couldn't wait to see the look on Meka's face when him and Baby found her.

When Tameka was dead, he would be at peace with Jean's death, but not a minute before.

His mind constantly thought of ways to kill her, but knowing that Baby wanted to more only made it easier. He was determined not to get his hands dirty, as always. Twan did his dirty work before and now his woman would too. It was only right, since they had plotted his demise anyway.

Getting Baby out of jail would ensure that she kept her mouth closed about his plan and her killing Tameka herself would seal that coffin. Then Gino could find his family and move on with his life.

"So you find out where your kid is?" Remy asked, when Gino nodded her eyes shined with excitement, causing him to chuckle. "Oh yes! Did he get a name?"

"Nah," Gino said. "Not a picture of him, but one of Cam leaving work and their apartment building."

"Dope," Remy asked. "So we headed there after the first?"

"I'm headed there after the first," he said. Remy frowned and sucked her teeth.

"What? Why?"

"Can I meet my kid first before I bring him around the crazy house?"

"…That was uncalled for," she said with her hand on her hip.

"It was real."

"I get it, G," Remy said. "You gonna act like Jean with her?"

"I ain't really decided yet," he admitted. "Might be easier than the truth."

"A lie is always easier," Remy said. "Just ain't right."

"Now you Oprah?"

"More like Iyanla," she said, laughing at her own joke. Gino just eyed her. "I'm low key excited though. I didn't think your plan was gonna work."

"What?"

"They believed you were a twin real quick."

"I am a twin."

"You know what I mean."

Gino laughed at Remy before telling her to get out of his room. Remy sucked her teeth and told him he was rude while walking out.

If Camryn hadn't of known that she was at Nana's house for Christmas, she would have thought she was dreaming when she woke up. Besides being in a strange bed with Ian's foot in her face, she could smell Nana's pancakes as if she was sleeping in the kitchen.

"It's Christmas!" Cam sang, looking over to see Ian up and staring at the ceiling. "You tell them angels Merry Christmas, baby?" she asked. He finally looked at her and giggled.

At the last minute, Cam decided to get a flight out to Nana's for Christmas. She had packed a few of Ian's gifts and caught a flight out last night. Mia had gone home with Jeremiah and she didn't want to celebrate Christmas alone.

Although Nana's sister had a house full, they were excited to have them there, more so Ian than Camryn. Auntie Mae, as Cam called her, was only about two years younger than Nana, but she had three kids. One of them, Emil, his wife Alyssa and their two kids stayed in the basement after he lost his job. They had two boys; Emil Jr and Ryan.

Cam snuggled up to the pillows while wondering if she should give Ian a bath before they ate. Although this wasn't their old home, the familiar smell of Nana's room was there. It made Cam feel safe and it was just what she needed.

Cam was glad that Nana had her own bathroom. She washed Ian up and got him dressed before brushing her own teeth and taming her hair. When she made it to the kitchen, everyone was about to sit down and eat.

"Good morning," she said, kissing Nana and Auntie Mae on the cheek. "You could have woke me up."

"You good child," Auntie Mae said. "We just finished cooking."

"Man, you look like your momma," Emil said, walking past her and taking Ian out of her hands. Cam smiled.

"You said that last night."

"And it's still true."

"Put that boy down, he has to learn how to walk before his birthday," Nana said.

"We got plenty of time for that," Emil said, kissing Ian's cheeks. Cam smiled once Ian started laughing and pulling on Emil's beard.

"Can we eat so we can open our gifts?" EJ said, bouncing in his seat.

"Pray over the food, Alyssa," Auntie Mae said.

It was nice being around family. Cam was less anxious knowing that Nana was being taken care of and not a burden on anyone. Auntie Mae confided in Cam they she did have a short hospital visit a few months ago that Nana didn't tell her about, but she only stayed two days. Cam told Auntie Mae she thought about moving closer to them, but Auntie Mae stopped her.

"I got my sister," she said. "You live your life."

When they began opening presents, the older boys were very excited while Ian just kind of looked on. He was more interested in the boxes and wrappers than his actual gifts. Cam took a few pictures of him on her phone while she sat with Alyssa.

"Anniversary coming up," Cam said.

"Yes!" Alyssa said. "11 years. Thanks for remembering."

"Y'all the only married couple I know…"

"Well, technically, Nana is still married and you can't tell her any different."

Cam laughed. "That's true…any big plans?"

"A weekend without the kids."

Ian crawled up to Cam and tapped her foot repeatedly. She smiled before sliding down next to him, leaning her back against the couch.

"You want Mommy to play?" she asked, taking the toy that he was handing to her. He looked up and smiled before pushing some of the wrapping paper into her lab while tearing it up. Cam looked at the toy he handed her and realized it was the phone she bought him since he was always trying to mess with hers. "Hello. You want to speak with Ian? Ian Mikel? Okay, hold on."

Cam put the phone up to his ear. Alyssa laughed as Ian stopped playing and held the phone as if someone was talking to him. He started laughing out of nowhere and in turn, Cam laughed too.

"Silly boy."

Nana and Auntie Mae came in after cleaning the kitchen and opened their gifts. Cam was glad to be around family, even if she didn't see them often. She didn't have that uneasy feeling she had been having at home, but she figured she just needed a break. After a few days with Nana, everything would go back to normal.

Lori frowned when she opened the door to see Remy there, smiling as if they were friends.

"...Can I help you with something?"

"Yes," Remy said, walking in past her. "Oh, your house is nice."

Lori sighed before closing the door. She turned around to see Remy sitting on the end of her couch.

"Please don't sit on my couch like that."

Remy threw her hands up and smirked. "My bad." She sat down on the couch and crossed her legs, bouncing them left to right while smiling up at Lori. "You look nice today."

"What do you want?"

"Tameka's number and address."

Lori laughed. "You can see yourself out."

"That's a shame...I wanted to tell you about my date with Moe last night."

Lori stopped her journey towards the kitchen and turned to look at Remy.

"He actually took you out?"

Remy laughed. "Why wouldn't he?"

"I...heard he has a girl..."

Remy laughed harder and nodded. "Oh you did, did you?"

Lori sat down on the love seat. "Where he take you?"

"Nice little restaurant up the way..."

"And?"

"We had a really nice time. He's so cute right?"

"He's...I mean, he's okay."

Remy frowned. "Ugh, you aren't even making this fun for me!" she pulled out a piece of paper and a pen and slammed it down on the table.

"What is that for?"

"Tameka's number and address before I go have a little talk with your baby daddy...and not the one whose baby you lost."

Lori's nose flared. "He told you that?"

"You're trifling...Chase is a good man," Remy said, shaking her head.

"Oh hush, like you have morals! Moe could be lying to you."

"Maybe, maybe not...but the way you just acted about our date and how y'all were looking at each other tells me he was for real."

Lori crossed her arms over her belly. "No one would believe you anyway."

Remy's left eyebrow raised as she smiled again. "You wanna test that little theory, bitch?"

Lori bit her lip as she frowned and thought of the possible outcome of Chase finding out that the loss of their baby, wasn't really his loss at all. The miscarriage before this pregnancy had been tough enough and although she was relived she didn't have to tell Chase about her and Moe, her heart hurt every time she thought of the baby girl.

Chase would kill Moe for sure. Lori might live because of their kids, but he'd definitely leave her. She might have gotten away with it if she would have cut Moe off when Chase first got out of jail. She had no excuse.

And what had Meka really done for Lori anyway, besides leave her?

But Chase was already skeptical of Jean and Remy. He hadn't come out right and said anything, but Lori could tell that Chase was ready for them to leave because he didn't trust him. There was no way he'd trust that Remy knew anything about her. If it came down to it, Chase would take her word over Remy's any day and that was something she was sure of.

Remy clapped her hands as Lori snatched the paper off the table tore it up.

"You need to leave," Lori said.

"Watch it," Remy said, standing. "Keep talking big, you've already made your own grave. I'm going to enjoy ending you."

Lori stepped back. "This is done. You won't get anything from me and try to talk to my man and I'll end you."

"Oh, fiesty!" Remy said with wide, excited eyes. "And here I thought you weren't any fun."

Lori stood up, holding her belly with one hand and pointing to her front door with the other. Remy smiled and walked out.

Baby stretched in her cell as the officer on duty came around with mail. She never really got any, so all she could think about was getting out to get some exercise. She stayed in the yard as much as possible to clear her mind.

She had been waiting a couple of weeks for Jean to contact her and she was starting to believe that it was all some trick to get information out of her. She was upset with herself for telling him what she knew, but also worried that if he did come through for her and found out she didn't know where Tameka was, she'd be dead.

"Jackson."

Baby looked up and frowned at the sound of her last name.

"What?"

"Somebody likes you today," the officer said, handing her an envelope. Baby looked at it but didn't reach to get it. Her cell mate laughed as the officer dropped it on the ground and kept moving.

"What is it?"

"How I'm supposed to know," Baby said, finally picking it up. "It says its from somebody's attorney's office."

She snatched the envelope open and began to read the letter. She hadn't really understood it, but the part that she could comprehend said that some new evidence had been brought up in her case and there was an appeal date set to get her charges dropped based on reasonable doubt.

"Oh my God! I gotta use the phone."

Gino laughed when he saw the number to the correctional facility pop up on his phone. It was a few days after the new year and he was feeling good about how his plan was going so far. His lawyer back home had put in the appeal for Baby with proof of him being alive. Since Meka's story was that "Gino" killed Twan and Baby killed "Gino" out of anger, all he had to do was prove that he was alive, which wasn't hard. Baby would need to give another testimony of how they killed each other, omitting the truth that Meka actually killed Twan. They didn't want her in jail. They had other plans for her.

"I don't know how you did it, but I owe you," Baby said.

"I told you I had it all figured out."

Baby sighed. "I can't even think straight right now. Is this real?"

"Just working on trying to move the hearing date up."

"There's something else I gotta tell you...about that night," Baby whispered.

"I need to come up there?"

"No," Baby said. "It happened before I got to the house."

"What?"

"Chase helped Meka break in me and Twan's spot. I don't know if he knew what she had going on, but he was the one who tied me up and put me in that truck."

Gino sighed. "Why you didn't tell me when I was up there?"

"I was still in shock honestly," Baby said. "You gotta admit how this doesn't seem like real life."

"Yeah, well it is."

"You think he had something to do with her set up?"

"I'll find out," Gino said.

Chase and Baywood watched Gino as he walked up the stairs towards the porch where they sat.

"How's business?" he asked. Baywood and Chase looked at each other and laughed. "What?"

"G always said that."

Gino laughed. "Got it honest."

Baywood nodded and looked towards the empty chair, letting Gino know that he could sit down.

"You get what you needed from Baby?" Baywood asked. He looked around the semi-empty street and nodded. "Still trying to piece some things together. That's actually why I'm here."

Baywood sighed. "Well, I wasn't there that night so it's not much I can help with."

"You weren't," Gino said. "But he was."

They both looked at Chase, who kept looking down at the blunt he was rolling.

"You were there?" Baywood asked. Chase glanced at him before back down at his handy work.

"Nah…" Chase started. Gino's nose flared.

"I call bullshit!" he said. "You been itching to get me away but didn't want to tell everything you knew! What you hiding?" he snapped. Baywood held his hand up, asking Gino to chill. Chase cut his eyes at him, but smirked.

"I said nah, but if you would have let me finish, I was going to say I saw Meka and Baby that night."

"What happened?" he asked. Chase's nose flared a little, hating to be questioned.

"Meka came up to the cash house saying how Twan and Baby was the snakes and we needed to move on them before it got worse. I couldn't find you," Chase said to Baywood. "So we went to Twan's spot by ourselves. When we got there he was already gone but Baby was there."

"Why you just now telling me?" Baywood asked.

"Baby locked up, Meka is gone, and Twan and G dead…what would be the point?"

"What happened after that?" Gino asked. Knowing that Chase was around Twan put him on edge. Was he one of the men that Baby said they had gotten on their side before everything went down? He had done a lot for Chase and at this point Gino's blood began to boil at the thought of Chase betraying him.

"Meka jumped on Baby after we broke the door down. I tied her up and put her in the truck. Meka said she had it from there and that G was waiting on her at home."

"You didn't think it was weird that G didn't come with her?" He asked. Chase sighed, heavily frustrated.

"I didn't think nothing."

Baywood shook his head. "Man…"

"I said what I know and that's all I know. I'm tired of this dude running around thinking he Gino and questioning everybody. We risked our lives for him daily and didn't even know about you."

"So you wasn't getting paid?" Gino asked.

"Man, I'm done talking to you."

"Don't act like you was a slave! You got bread just like everybody else! Who looked out for you and your ratchet ass baby momma while you were locked up? Huh?"

"This nigga really think he's Gino!" Chase said.

It was as if Gino snapped at the mention of his own name. For weeks, he had been answering to Jean, taking on the persona of his fallen twin to get more information without spooking everyone around. For weeks, he had to tame himself silently instead of running through the streets shooting everyone he thought might have betrayed him like he wanted to. For weeks, he had to be civil to Lori, someone he could never stand the sight of, just to see what she knew about his estranged wife.

He was tired of it all.

Before anyone could blink, Gino had pulled out a pistol and struck Chase on the side of his temple, hard and quick. He groaned in pain, the force pushing him back out of the chair but Gino didn't let him get far. He was on top of him, hitting him repeatedly in the head with the butt of his gun before Chase's body hit the ground and Baywood could get him off.

"Come on, man!" Baywood yelled, wondering why he couldn't pull him off. He hadn't looked as strong as he was, but Baywood was having a hard time.

"All that talk for what?" Gino yelled in Chase's face. He grinned to see Chase spitting out blood. "Run your mouth now, punk!"

"That's enough!" Baywood said, finally getting Gino off him. He had to brace himself when Chase struggled to get up and charged after Gino with whatever strength he had left.

"Y'all just need to chill," Baywood said, trying to diffuse the situation. "I'm sure that's all he knows."

"Is that all you know?" Gino snapped. Chase looked at him for a moment. The pain from his busted lip was throbbing, but he tried to stand up as tall as possible. He wanted to kill dude, but Chase knew it wouldn't be an easy task. His nose flared and his chest heaved up and down a few times before he nodded, but that didn't satisfy his opponent. "Is that all Lori knows?"

"Yeah, man…"

Gino decided to let the conversation die. He never liked Lori and he knew if he kept talking or if Chase tried to defend her, he'd end up telling it all just because. Out of respect for Chase, he left it alone. Chase had done a bid and not told on anyone while he was locked up. Gino would let him be ignorant to the fact that his woman was ratchet.

He looked at Chase for a second longer before turning to leave. The high he felt from seeing blood rush from Chase's nose and lip hadn't gone un-noticed.

EIGHT

Cam was at the end of her rope. She had worked ten days straight and finally had two off. Although she had spent the first one lounging around the house, she figured today she would take Ian to the park since it was nice out. That was one advantage to living in the south.

It was only a week into January and Cam had been stressing about Ian's birthday. Nana wasn't well enough to get on a plane. Cam just decided that she and Mia would host a party at Ian's daycare and then a small dinner at home. She had already gotten it approved. At first, she had wanted to have a big party, but Ian wouldn't remember any of it.

She had been trying to get him to walk for the last couple of weeks, so she figured the park was a good place to practice. Lots of grass.

She smiled as he fought to get out of her hands when he figured out where they were. The park wasn't very big. It had a small basketball court and a few swing sets.

What Cam liked about the park was the mini set in the middle for toddlers. Although Ian wasn't quite a toddler yet, he did like to play in the sand box there. Cam made sure to look around for anything that could hurt him and even sat in the sand box with him when they were there. The park also had a few toddler swings that strapped them in, but Ian didn't care for them that much.

Cam laughed as he pushed both of his stubby little hands into the sand and threw some up in the air.

"Sorry it's been so long since we been here, son," she said, sitting on the edge of the sandbox in front of him. She put his bucket down in front of him and he crawled over to it. "I wish you'd walk."

Cam took a few pictures and small videos while playing with Ian. Spending time with him always put her in a better mood. She thought about random stuff, but mostly his future. What would he sound like when he talked? Would he stay her color or would he get a little darker and match his father's color?

Cam shook her head at her line of thinking as Ian put his little shovel in her hand.

"We need some friends, son," she said, giggling.

"You plan on him talking back?"

Cam frowned and prepared to turn around and address whoever was talking to her. She put her hands on the side and turned to look. The air left her lungs and her heart dropped. She immediately got a headache as possible explanations swarmed her brain. She had visions before of her mother when she was pregnant, but this was something totally different. The man standing just a few feet from her could not be standing there at all when he was buried a year ago.

After her initial shock, Cam jumped up and grabbed Ian, leaving his toys in the sandbox. She tried to jump out of it, but her foot got caught in the sand. She screamed as she felt herself falling with Ian in her arms. Cam froze when the man caught her. Once she got her footing she backed up.

"Don't touch me."

"Camryn, calm down. I'm his twin, you aren't hallucinating."

"Gino doesn't have a twin...what are you?"

Gino licked his lips and laughed a little before pulling a picture out of his pocket. It was of him and Jean at their high school graduation. He held it out for Cam to see. She leaned forward and squinted while trying to sooth Ian, who was now crying.

"Identical twin?" Cam questioned aloud. When he didn't answer she looked up to see him staring at Ian. She held him tighter and cleared her throat.

"Jean," he said, not taking his eyes off the baby. "What's his name?"

"...Ian Mikel."

"He looks like me."

"I have to go," Cam said, trying to rush off again. Her heart felt like it would leap out of her chest.

"Wait...Camryn, just wait a second. I didn't mean to push this all on you," he said, handing her the picture. "My number is on the back...."

Cam took the picture and headed to the car quickly. Ian, being able to tell something was bothering his mother, continued to cry.

"It's okay baby," Cam said, strapping him in. "I got you."

Cam got in the car, turned it on, and locked all the doors. Deciding not to go home just yet, she drove around to calm down a little before stopping at a local diner to call Nana. She didn't want to go home just yet just in case Jean was still around.

Gino parked in the lot across from Cam's apartment building and lit his pre-rolled blunt. His heart had been pounding since he walked up to Cam and his son at the park. He kept thinking about the night he took her to the hospital and felt him kick in her belly.

He wanted to admit the truth to her the minute he saw her. He wanted to kiss her, hug her, play with his son. He wanted to be with her and all those feelings he had for her came running back.

"This is harder than I thought," he said to himself, looking at her parking space. He smirked, knowing that she wouldn't come straight home. He'd found her place a few days ago and had been keeping an eye on her. Wanted to make sure she didn't have a man he'd have to get rid of. He had promised Granny Watson that he wouldn't kill anyone, but he was pretty sure she knew that was a promise he was willing to break if need be.

"Ian Mikel…"

Gino couldn't explain what it felt like to see his son. Guilt riddled his body at the thought of trying to end his life before it began. He looked like him as a baby and the fact that Camryn actually remembered that he'd told her he had a brother whose middle name was Mikel had blown him away. He had lied to her and said he died when he was younger, and Gino never really understood why he'd come up with that lie about Jean, but she remembered and used that name for their son.

He laughed at nothing in particular before calling Granny Watson.

"Hello, Grandson."

He frowned. "Why you answer the phone like that?"

"Because I'm bored and it's your fault," she said. Gino laughed.

"I love you though, I brought Remy back."

"She's no fun, that girl is too much. Anyway, did you find them yet."

"I did."

"Praise God!" she said. "Bring them home."

Gino laughed. "It's not that simple, Ma."

"She thinks your Jean too, huh?"

He sighed. "It's the easiest way to gain access. I can't tell her the truth that quick."

"I don't think it'll be any easier for her either way, son."

Gino listened to his grandmother talk about why impersonating his dead twin wasn't sitting well in her spirit when he noticed Cam's car pull up in her spot. He zoned out, keeping in eye on her to gauge how she was moving. Her hair was in a ponytail now, which means she probably got hot. She used to do that when she was nervous about something. She quickly got out of the car and pulled Ian from the back seat. Gino shook his head. She didn't even look around her surroundings before going in the house.

"Gino!"

"Yes ma'am."

"Goodbye..."

Gino laughed as she hung up on him. He knew he'd have to sweet talk her later, but he had to focus. He'd introduced himself and now, as much as he didn't want to, he had to wait for Cam to make the next move.

Cam closed her eyes as she let Nana process what she'd just told her. Her spirit wasn't settled when she got home, so she called her back. Nana was the only one she trusted to listen without judgement.

"A twin, huh?" Nana asked.

"He looks a lot like him," Cam admitted. "Besides him being a little skinner and facial hair..."

"Wow. Who would have saw that coming?"

"Nana, be serious."

"I know this is a lot for you baby, but you have to call him."

"Why?" Cam asked, shocked at Nana's response.

"From what you told me, Gino didn't have a lot of family and they are probably very eager to meet Ian."

"...You think that's safe."

"I don't see what would be wrong with it."

"I don't know," Cam admitted. "There has to be a reason Gino never told me he had a twin."

"Now that part is a little shady, but there were a lot of things he didn't tell you."

Cam sucked her teeth. "You're right. I wonder how he found me."

"How about you talk to him a little more and get your questions answered," Nana suggested. "It may ease your mind a little more about him being around Ian."

"That sounds feasible," Cam said.

"So are you going to call him?"

Cam looked down at the picture he had given her and sighed. "Not today."

Tameka sat at her cubicle, biting the tip of her right thumb nail staring off into space. She had tried to call Lori three times with no reply. She usually wouldn't trip, but in light of the last conversation she'd had with her best friend, she was a little paranoid.

Tameka racked her brain for the last few weeks, trying to make sense of Gino having an identical twin that she didn't know about. She was just getting comfortable in her new home and here Gino was, still disrupting her life.

"Can't run from you," Tameka mumbled, shaking the mouse of her computer to keep it from falling asleep. She wasn't fond of her call center job, but it was boring and normal.

Just what she needed.

"Carla….Carla….Miss Delaney."

"Yes…" Tameka said, looking up at her boss.

"Are you okay?"

"Yes, sorry."

"There are calls in the queue."

"…Right."

Tameka rolled her eyes as soon as he walked away, looking at the clock to see how much time she had left in her day. She wanted to get home before Marcus did and make dinner for him. Tameka smiled, thinking of how Marcus always came home on time and always let her know where he was.

Very different from her dead husband.

Tameka met Marcus a few months after she moved to Savannah, Georgia. She changed her name to Carla Delaney and applied for a job at the call center while stashing her money away in a bank account. Marcus worked in construction and met her outside of her job where she ate lunch at. They dated about five months before moving in together.

He centered her. He loved her and listened to her and was more than excited to have a baby with her. Marcus was everything Gino wasn't and it was why everyday Tameka felt her heart breaking at keeping a secret from him. She was hoping to get over it soon.

After work, Tameka smiled as she made it to an empty home. She quickly made her way to the kitchen to see what she would cook for dinner. Marcus was very health-conscious and didn't eat any fried foods. Deciding she would grill some fish and shrimp, Tameka pulled the seafood out of the freezer and set it in the sink to unthaw.

While preparing everything else, she decided to try and call Lori again. To her surprise, she answered.

"What's up? Where you been?" Tameka asked.

"What you mean?"

"I called you like three times."

"...Oh, stuff been crazy around here. The twins got suspended from daycare and my doctor has me on bedrest for two weeks."

"Everything okay with the baby?" Tameka asked, not one hundred percent sold on the story.

"Yeah, my blood pressure up, that's all."

"Oh, well chill out," Tameka laughed.

"What's up?" Lori asked. Tameka frowned.

"What you mean? I haven't talked to you in weeks."

"I'm cool, Meka," Lori said. Tameka could tell she had an attitude.

"What's up with the attitude, Lori? That so called twin still snooping around?"

"Nah...he's gone."

"Good. You seen Tani?"

"I don't ever see her," Lori said with a snicker. "What you doing?"

"Cooking dinner."

"Well, let me get some rest before Chase comes back with these kids."

Lori pretty much hung up before Tameka could say anything. She sighed, knowing that something went down and she'd have to stop calling Lori to be sure. Tameka didn't know what Gino's twin was up to, but she wanted no parts of it.

"I'm thinking crazy," she said, laughing at herself. Baby was in jail and she was the only other person who could say anything about that night and actually tell the truth.

She shook her head while she continued to cook. The alarm sounded and her heart skipped a beat. Within minutes, the strongest arms she'd ever been comfortable in wrapped around her waist.

"I missed you all day," Marcus said, pushing his lips into her neck.

"You're just hungry," Tameka said. Marcus laughed before kissing the side of her head and tapping her butt before walking away.

"I'm going to clean up before dinner."

"It should be done in about twenty minutes," she called after him.

Baby hadn't been in jail that long for things to seem so different, but during her bus ride home that was all she could think about. Businesses and places she was used to seemed to be closed and no one around the block looked familiar.

"Guess that's a good thing," she mumbled as her stop neared. She knew she'd have to walk a couple of blocks but she welcomed the air and time to think. Everything had happened so quickly and she still wasn't sure what to do outside of her main focus of handling Tameka for pinning the murder on her.

"Can't wait to see the look on her face," Baby said, laughing to herself. Her head was swimming with the details of her release. Knowing Gino was alive made her a little skeptical of his actual plans for her, but since he'd gotten her out of jail, she'd keep his secret and ride the plan out. She had to figure out a way to insure her safety after she killed Tameka. Gino would have no use for her then and Baby was sure that he hadn't forgotten that she was helping Twan take over the business.

Baby couldn't wait to get to her mother's house. She knew her mouth wouldn't be welcoming, but the shower and bed that awaited her would be.

Baby's walk home from the bus stop wasn't half bad until she passed Twan's old house. It was the one he was in before they got that condo downtown together. She smiled as she remembered watching him for weeks before making her move. He tried to act as if he wasn't phased by her attention and that made Baby want him more.

Baby's throat got dry as she thought about all the nights they stayed up, planning their take over. They had fun together and she missed him a lot. She couldn't help but feel as if his death was her fault.

"If I would have just kept my mouth closed," Baby mumbled to herself, tearing her eyes away from the house and briskly walking past it. Her sadness morphed into anger at Tameka as it always did. Almost every night that she had been locked up, Baby ran that night back in her head and always wanted to kick herself for going to Tameka and Gino's house. Yes, she was mad at Twan for hitting her, but she had spoiled their plan. Both of them were paranoid that it wouldn't be too long before Gino had someone come shoot up their condo.

Baby sat on the couch with a lit cigarette in hand, biting her lip and tapping her bare foot against the base of the marble living room table. She had been home for twenty minutes, and she had to admit that she was a little nervous about Twan's reaction to her telling Tameka about their plan.

A lapse in judgment, Baby admitted, was what happened. She had been watching Tameka for so long that she was sure there was a method to her marrying Gino so quickly. The way Tameka reacted at Red Lobster's left Baby confused. She knew that Tameka would get to Twan before she did, and now her man was pissed at her.

She had possibly messed up the plan and cost them their lives.

Baby heard the door slam and shivered. She had heard stories of what Twan did to people, but she had never seen him in action. She didn't think he would do anything to her.

But she had her razor tucked securely under her tongue anyway.

Twan's heavy steps fell against the carpet as he made his way through the condo, on a silent rampage.

Baby straightened her back just before he walked into the living room.

"Do you know what you've done?" Twan said, huffing his words out in short breaths.

"She figured it out before I even opened my mouth, boo," Baby said. Twan raised his hand to silence her. Baby's nose flared, but she said nothing.

"You think you know everything. I can't believe how stupid and naïve you're being," Twan went on, his face getting redder by the second. "That's his wife, Tati, his damn wife! The person that will do anything for him, and you told her what was going on?!"

"Will you calm down? If she was going to tell him, she would have told him before even letting us know that she knew!" Baby said, pushing her back against the couch.

Twan huffed again, took two steps and had Baby up against the wall by her neck. She winced in pain; the way he grabbed her made her lose control of her blade, and it cut into the inside of her jaw and under her tongue.

"From now on, you don't make a move until I tell you to. Don't speak to no one, look at no one, or think about nothing until I tell you to, do you understand?" Twan said into her cheek. Baby groaned, but tried not to show that she was in pain.

Twan frowned and stretched his arm out, pushing Baby into the wall more and putting distance between their bodies. The blood running down the side of her mouth made Twan's nose flare.

He pushed her jaws together and Baby yelped as the blade cut her more. He pulled it out of her mouth and threw it on the coffee table.

"So... you were going to cut me?"

Before Baby could answer, Twan had backslapped her onto the couch. Baby scrambled to her feet to fight back, but as soon as she got her footing, Twan's open hand slid across her other cheek.

"You think you bad, Baby?!" Twan asked as he continued to beat her. Baby's punches only could do so much. They seemed to only make him hit her harder.

"Stop!" Baby finally pleaded, and immediately he did. Twan dropped Baby on the couch and walked away.

It took Baby ten minutes to clean as much blood off of her face as she could to look presentable before she slid some shades on and left. Fifteen minutes after that, she was sitting in front of Gino and Tameka's.

She silently cursed, seeing all the cars home before pulling her phone out and dialing Tameka's number.

"Hello?" Tameka answered.

"We need to talk," Baby said, lighting a cigarette.

"Where are you?" Tameka asked. Baby closed her eyes before slamming her head into the headrest, mad at herself for getting into this situation.

"I'm outside."

Baby should have known that Tameka was up to something, but she couldn't do anything about it now. Twan was dead and he wasn't coming back, but sending Meka to a similar grave would sure help her feel a hell of a lot better.

When Baby finally made it home, she knocked on the front door quickly and shifted her back to her other shoulder. Her mother's heavy footsteps could be heard on the other side of the door, so she took a deep breath to prepare herself for the lecture that was coming.

"Praise God," Janetta, Baby's mother said as she swung the screen door open. Baby smiled, happy to see her mom despite the circumstances. It had been a couple of months since she visited.

"Hey Ma," Baby said, moving past her and into the house. She put her bag down before turning around to hug her. Janetta put her hand up and shook her head.

"Take a bath first child, don't want those jail house germs on me."

Baby rolled her eyes and laughed, knowing that was what she expected from her mom but took her advice anyway. She could hear people moving around the house but decided to go straight to her room and get settled before trying to greet anyone else.

Her room was cold. She wasn't sure what felt different, but she immediately knew she'd have to get some money and get her own place soon. Baby wondered if the team had found all of Twan's cash stashes by now. She knew her mom found hers because she told her she did. Baby wasn't even mad about it. She felt numb about everything.

After her shower, she walked around her room and felt her heart breaking again. Jewelry that Twan had purchased, pictures of them on her dresser, CDs that she had lying around that they used to ride and listen to together. Her car keys sat on the dresser and she knew the car he'd bought her was in the garage. That was one thing she didn't bend on. No one was allowed to drive the car and she knew where the mileage was when she left.

Baby slid her hand across one picture in particular and picked it up before sitting down on the edge of her bed. They were at a party and her friend had taken the picture. She was looking down smiling, while Twan was behind her with one hand around her waist and another holding her neck. She was laughing because he was biting her cheek in the picture. She remembered telling him that he needed to stop biting her before people thought he was a cannibal. He referenced his favorite part of her to nibble on before biting her cheek to demonstrate.

Baby couldn't help the tears and since she wasn't around a bunch of women who would try and hurt her if she showed weakness, she finally let them fall. No matter what people thought of her and Twan, they loved the hell out of each other. The guilt of her part in ruining that bond was eating her alive.

"Tati!" Janetta yelled from the other side of the door. "Come on and speak to everybody, child!"

"Yes ma'am, give me a second," she yelled back, tossing the picture on the dresser and searching for something that fit. She shook her head, knowing that her cousins probably ransacked her drawers the first chance they got. The only thing that looked decent was a pair of yoga pants and a few of her plain tee shirts.

She put her wet hair up in a bun, grabbed a pair of socks and left out of her bedroom. The first person she ran into was her Aunt Kayla.

"Hey Auntie," she said, hugging her.

"You use every drop of hot water on the block?" she joked, patting her back. Baby laughed. "I didn't believe it, but I'm glad you're home."

"I told y'all I didn't do it," Baby mumbled, walking past her into the living room where her cousins were. They all stood up to hug her.

"Well, every murderer says they didn't do it," one of her cousins said. She ignored them. They were always jealous of her when she was out, so nothing there had changed.

"Ma, did you cook?"

"I did. Made a pizza, it's almost done. Keisha drove your car to the store."

"No, she didn't."

"How come I didn't?" Keisha asked. Baby's nose flared.

"I told you not to let anyone drive my car," Baby said, looking directly at her mom.

"Well, baby I don't see what the big deal is. Plus, the pizza was for you."

Baby tried to control her breathing as she got up, ran back to her room and grabbed her keys. She went out the kitchen door into the garage and swung the door open. She bit her lip while looking at her candy red Cadillac and how dusty it looked.

"I'm going to beat her ass if she drove my car," Baby said to herself, opening the driver's door. She turned the key and waited impatiently for the mileage to pop up. She rolled her eyes and relaxed in the seat. Looking up at the garage door, she saw Keisha laughing. Baby gave her the finger, but couldn't help but laugh.

Gino wiped his hands down the front of his jeans as he stood outside Cam's door. It had been about a week since he'd introduced himself to her as Jean and he had to admit that he expected her to call him sooner.

He was surprised but proud that she was taking more precautions with her safety and ultimately their son's. When he first started dealing with Cam, she was very careless and naive, except when it came to her Nana. She was raised differently than any other woman he had been with. Gino guessed that was part of the reason he fell for her.

He had been eager to get back home and figure out his plan of action in helping Baby get Tameka when Cam called and agreed to let him spend time with Ian. He had no idea how he'd be able to keep his secret, but he had to be near them by any means necessary.

Gino looked up when Cam opened the door and tried not to bit his lip at how good she looked.

"Hey Jean, come on in," Cam said, stepping aside.

He waited until she closed the door to speak. "Thanks for calling me," he said, noticing she didn't lock the front door, but decided not to say anything.

"Well, I have my reservations," Cam said. "But you are his uncle and he deserves to know his family."

"I appreciate that, where is he?"

Cam sighed. "In his room, follow me."

Gino bit his lip before nodding, following Cam through the apartment. He was eager to see Ian, but frowned when they walked in and he was sleep.

"He should be up soon," Cam said, reading his facial expressions. "I figured this would give us a chance to talk."

"What about?"

"I am open to letting you in Ian's life, but I need to feel more comfortable around you so I have some questions," Cam said, walking back into the living room.

Gino frowned. "I'm not trying to hurt you or Ian."

"I know that," Cam said, honestly. "But I still have questions."

He was beginning to get annoyed, but sat down silently and waited for her to speak again.

"You stay in the same place as Granny Watson?" she asked. He nodded. "Why didn't she come with you?

"She's old. Wanted to make sure you were up for sharing him before she made a trip."

"Why wait so long?" she asked.

"…We didn't take Gino's death well," he said above a whisper. "Still not taking it well. Being close to Ian will help."

Cam nodded subconsciously, knowing that Ian was her saving grace in that way as well.

"Any other relatives that might pop up?"

Gino bit his lip and glared at her for a moment. "Nah, just us two."

Cam felt uncomfortable in that moment with how he looked at her. What made it more strange was he didn't look away once she noticed it. The way he looked at her made her forget her next question.

"Anything else you wanna know?"

"Oh um…what about your parents?"

He gave her a blank stare. "What about them?"

"Gino never mentioned them when we were..dating," Cam said, trying to find the right word. "Just wondered."

"Old man is doing a life bid," he said quickly.

"Oh my God," Cam said. "Why."

"Killing our mom."

" ... "

" ... "

"Okay, that's enough questions. I'm sure Ian is up by now," she said, standing quickly and almost stumbling over her feet to get out of the living room. Gino smirked and tried not to laugh, knowing that his answer caught her off guard.

He looked around the living room while Cam was gone, trying to see if she had any pictures up with another man. His blood always boiled at the thought of her being with anyone else. He had been very possessive of her ever since he took her virginity.

Gino nodded his head victoriously as Twan handed Baywood the duffle bag of money they'd just counted. This week had been a good one. Not only was business booming, but Tameka hadn't been bothering him and Cam had agreed to spend the night with him in the suite he'd gotten downtown.

He hadn't told any of his boys about him and Cam and up until today it hadn't been much to tell. After she finally let him take her to eat after school months ago, it became their little ritual on Fridays. Her graduation was next weekend and since he couldn't be there for her publicly, he had to spoil her today.

Gino had given her money to get her nails done and a sew-in. He asked why she did it so early and she told him so her head wouldn't be sore on graduation day. He knew with her Nana being sick, she would need a distraction and he had the perfect one.

"Alright, I'm out," Gino said to his team before heading outside to his truck. Cam had just sent him a picture of her hair, letting him know she was on her way home to get dressed. Gino smiled, his plan was running smoothly. As long as Tameka stayed mad and not speaking to him, it would be a good night.

Gino made a few stops around the block until Cam said she was ready. When he pulled up she ran out of the door.

"What you running from?" he asked, laughing as she got in. Her smile warmed his cold heart every time.

"Nothing...I just was excited to see you," she admitted.

"You better be," he said. Cam rolled her eyes and he slid his hand around the back of her neck, moving her to kiss him. He smirked once he pulled away, seeing her with her bottom lip between her teeth and her eyes closed. She peeked at him and sucked her teeth.

"You so low," she said, sitting back and putting her seatbelt on. Gino laughed and put the car in drive.

"This room is too much," Cam said, squealing as she kicked her shoes off and began running around the living room area. Gino watched her in amusement. Cam was

very mature for her age, but times like these reminded him she was a month shy of 18.

"Come here," he said. Cam stopped in her tracks and walked back to where he stood. She grinned as he wrapped his arms around her waist and she kissed him.

"This your last chance to back out," he said against her lips. Cam laughed.

"I'm ready," she said. "Just take it slow with me."

Hearing Cam's voice come around the corner knocked Gino out of his daydream. He had to clear his throat and try to regain control. Thinking of their time together made it hard for him not to act on his desire for her. Now wasn't the time.

"Son, you have company," Cam said. Gino watched the miniature version of himself lay his head on Cam's chest and eye him, almost protectively. He smirked. "This is your Uncle Jean."

Gino's heart hurt a little at the introduction, but it hurt worse when he reached for Ian and he turned away.

"What's wrong?" he said, panicking as the baby began to cry.

"Nothing," Cam said with a reassuring smile. "He just has to get used to you." She sat down next to Gino and rubbed Ian's back. "Just give him a minute."

NINE

Cam signed as she looked around the inventory room and wanted to quit her job at that very moment. With school and the demands of being a part-time manager, she felt like she didn't have any time to spend with Ian. She thanked God that her and Mia's schedules worked out that he only had to go to a sitter three days a week, but she felt like as soon as they got home they went to sleep.

Cam had decided that after inventory she would take three days off work and spend time with Ian. She didn't have any classes during that time so she was excited. It would also be the first time since introducing Jean to Ian that she would allow him to come over and spend time with him.

She was still a little skeptical, but Jean had been answering her questions and even brought more pictures of him and Gino when they were younger that Cam could look at. Seeing how deep the resemblance was to them and Ian was crazy, but it helped her get more comfortable with him being around.

They hadn't talked much, but Jean would text and ask her questions about what Ian liked and disliked. What was his favorite food, when did he start walking, all of that. With Ian's birthday two weeks away, Cam was excited to have Nana come visit. Especially now so she could talk to her about this situation and get her real opinion on it.

She hadn't mentioned his birthday to Jean just yet. She remembered telling Gino when she was due, but didn't think anyone outside of her loved ones knew when Ian was actually born.

Finally finishing up her managerial duties, Cam clocked out and made her way to Mia's to pick Ian up.

"Hey suga," she said, kissing Mia's cheek when she opened the door.

"Ian just went to sleep," Mia said.

"Good, that means I can go to sleep," Cam said. If Ian was sleep by eight, that meant he'd stay sleep for the night. Cam got a little excited, thinking she could maybe read a few chapters of a book she had been attempting to finish.

"Hey, I need to talk to you before you head home," Mia said. Cam noted the tone in her voice and nodded before sitting at her table.

"What's up?"

"I talked to Mom today and apparently there is some news going around town about Jean coming back."

"He's been there?" Cam asked. Mia nodded. "Does he sell?"

"She didn't mention that, said he's been asking around about what happened to Gino. Also been looking at the house Gino and Tameka stayed in."

"Um," Cam asked.

Mia frowned. "Why do you think he'd be snooping around there?"

Cam laughed. "I wouldn't call it snooping. Maybe he just really wants to know what happened. We don't really know what happened. All the papers said was a deal gone bad and we know Gino never really got caught up in anything."

"Camryn, you serious?" Mia sucked her teeth. "Some things don't change I guess."

"Girl, you're tripping. That is my son's uncle. We are far from home and me and Tameka made our peace. I ain't tripping about what he did back there. I just want Ian to know his family. He has a right to."

"You have to protect him, Camryn."

"What is it you think I'm not doing?" Cam asked, frowning at her best friend.

Mia sighed. "I didn't mean it like that."

"What did you mean, Mia? I'm being cautious. Jean isn't doing anything but trying to get to know his nephew. He hasn't been pushy, disrespectful or anything. If I think otherwise, I'll shut it down. Okay?"

Cam didn't want to argue with Mia, but she was tired of everyone trying to run her life. She knew they meant well, but Cam had to do what was best for her and Ian and no one else could decide that for her.

Mia sighed and nodded. "Okay."

Cam nodded and tried to change the subject. "Okay, so Nana gets in Friday. I'm going to take the day off to make sure I'm available to get her, but she will be looking for you as well."

Mia laughed. "I work days next week so we're good."

"Cool. I'm going to cook for her so I'll need Jeremiah's help."

Mia laughed. "That'll be right up his alley."

"Tell him we don't need a five-star meal now, we on a budget."

They both laughed.

The next few days went by quickly as Cam prepared for Nana's visit and Ian's first birthday. She tried not to get emotional every time she thought about it, but knowing how rough it was getting him to the world only made it worse.

"We survived a year," she thought. "We may be okay after all."

"You say something?" Gino asked from the living room. Cam snapped out of her thoughts and continued to wash the greens in her sink.

"No, just mumbling. Y'all good?"

"We good."

Cam nodded, even though they couldn't see her. She had invited Jean over for dinner. He said he would be out of town for the next few days. Cam wanted to invite him to Ian's birthday get together. She also had a few more questions.

After she got the greens in the pot, Cam wiped her hands and joined the boys in the living room.

"When does Ian turn one?" he asked. Cam smiled.

"Next week. The day you turn 27."

Gino smiled. "Yeah? You had him on the 26th?"

Cam nodded. Gino laughed, proudly.

"I was actually wondering if Uncle Jean would be at his party?" Cam asked, sitting on the floor behind Ian.

"Of course, I'll be there," he said. He handed Ian a toy out of his reach and tickled his leg. Ian laughed and Gino smiled slowly.

"You're really good with him."

"This my little homie," Gino said. Cam laughed.

"I'm glad he has a chance to know you, to be honest I always felt bad that he wouldn't know his dad."

"Why? That's not your fault."

"Yeah, I feel like it is. If I hadn't of fallen in love with a self-centered, power hungry cheater." Gino winced. "Sorry, I know that's your brother. No offense."

Gino sighed. "I understand y'all relationship wasn't all good."

"It was mostly bad," Cam blurted out. "At least after I got pregnant."

"Yeah…"

"Sorry, didn't mean to bring that up."

"Stop apologizing, Camryn," he said. "It's what happened. Can't change it."

Cam bit her lip and nodded. The way he talked to her reminded her of Gino so much. Cam hated the way her stomach turned in a way that only Gino used to elicit. Cam shook the feeling off, not thinking much of it.

"How did people tell you all apart when you were younger?" Gino laughed. "What?"

"Nothing, that just made me think of the time J…I lost my virginity."

"Really?"

Gino sighed. "I had a little problem getting girls. Well, I didn't think it was a problem. Just wasn't into all that, but Gino was hell bent on changing that."

"What happened?"

"He tricked the head cheerleader into thinking she was about to sex him. Got her to the house and told me to go in the room."

"And you did it!?" Cam asked. "How old were y'all?"

"15."

Cam shook her head. "What happened? Y'all got away with it."

"Chick was sloppy drunk, didn't even know." Gino smiled at the memory, remembering how Jean acted afterwards and what Tina said about it afterwards, thinking they both shared that moment together as he walked her home.

"So y'all were those type of twins," Cam teased.

"The best at it."

They laughed before Cam stood up and went to check on the food. Once they sat down to eat, the conversation switched back to Ian's birthday.

"I usually spend my birthday with my godsister and Granny," Gino said. "You mind if I bring them to the party?"

Cam frowned. "Where is home exactly?"

"Upstate, only about an hour and half from here."

Cam nodded. "I was wondering how you get here so quick."

Gino laughed. "They've been bugging to meet him, but if you're not cool with it then…"

"No, it's fine. We don't have much family so having them here would be great."

Gino smiled at Cam. "Great."

Mia frowned in annoyance as she watched Cam run around the apartment.

"Camryn Charmaine, you need to calm down. He don't even know what's going on," Mia said, looking down at Ian as he slept next to her on the couch. Cam sighed as Nana walked in from the back room and agreed with Mia.

"This is his first birthday," Cam whined. "I want it to be special."

"It'll be special," Mia said.

"Child, go check on the food," Nana said, picking Ian up while gently coaxing him to wake. "I'll start getting him ready."

Cam briskly walked into the kitchen to stir the spaghetti and sighed when Mia walked in. "Do you think it's weird that there aren't any kids coming? I don't want my baby to be a loner."

Mia laughed. "Boo, you are over thinking this. We don't know many people up here with kids. He'll have plenty of time to get older, go to school and make friends to come to his birthday parties."

"You're right," Cam said. "Don't really know why I'm bugging anyway."

Mia nodded and Cam walked back in the kitchen to see Jeremiah now manning the stove.

"Hey Jeremiah," Cam said, walking into the kitchen. "You good in here?"

"Yes ma'am," he said. Cam laughed. "Hey, let me talk to you right quick."

"What's up?"

"Mia is a little worried about Ian's uncle being around," he said. Cam rolled her eyes and he sighed.

"I'm sure."

"No, just hear me out," he said, looking towards the door to make sure no one was coming in. "She wouldn't tell me everything, but I think she's scared he's going to hurt you."

Cam sighed. "Ian's dad and I went through a lot when I found out I was pregnant. Granted, it wasn't pretty, in the end I forgave him. Mia has to trust me. Besides, he's not Ian's dad, even if they look identical."

"You sure everything is okay?" he asked. "I'm the only man around here since Jayson left."

Cam rolled her eyes again. "We're good, Dad."

Jeremiah laughed it off. Cam heard a knock on the door and felt butterflies in her stomach. She was nervous. She smoothed her shirt down before walking through the living room to the front door. When she opened it, Cam was shocked to see who was at the door.

"Surprise!" Jayson said, holding up two big bags and balloons.

"What are you doing here?" Cam blurted out.

Jayson frowned. "It's Ian's birthday."

Cam sighed. "What are you doing in town?"

He looked at her for a moment. "…It's Ian's birthday."

"Surprise!" Mia said, moving to the door and gently pushing Cam aside. Cam looked at her, realizing that she knew Jayson was coming. "The gift table is up against the window."

Jayson nodded before walking in.

"Be nice," Mia said.

"Why didn't you tell me he was coming?"

"He wanted to surprise you."

Cam rolled her eyes. "Right."

"Who came in?" Nana asked from the bedroom. Jayson's face lit up.

"Is that Nana?" he asked. Cam had to laugh at his facial expression before she nodded.

Nana came out the room with Ian on her hip. Cam almost burst into tears. She had successfully put four braids in his hair that morning, which he never let her do. Mia had gotten him a black and red shirt made that said, "Ian's 1st Birthday!" in block letters to match his black and red Jordan's and light denim pants.

"Aw, son!" Cam said, taking him from Nana and hugging him to her chest. "Stop growing up!"

"Hey Jayson," Nana said, hugging him. "What a surprise!"

"You know I couldn't miss little man's birthday," he said, glancing at Cam. She rolled her eyes and bounced Ian on her hip.

"You gonna walk for Momma today?"

Mia laughed. "If you keep holding him, he won't."

Cam sighed but her heart jumped when someone knocked on the door again. "That should be them." She turned to head back to the door.

Jayson frowned. "Them who?"

Cam opened the door with a smile. "Hey!"

Gino smiled. "Look at the birthday boy!"

"Come in," Cam said, stepping aside. She smiled before looking behind him. "You must be Granny Watson."

Granny Watson stopped in front of her and Ian and burst into tears. Everyone in the room stopped.

"Oh God," Remy said, rubbing her back.

"Did I say something wrong?" Cam asked, holding onto Ian who had buried his face into her chest.

"Granny, you okay?" Gino asked, hoping she took their conversation in the car to heart. He was worried about her blowing his cover to Camryn. She still didn't understand why he hadn't revealed himself yet. She had no idea that finding Cam and Ian wasn't the only thing on his to-do list.

"I'm okay child, it's nice to see you again."

"Again?" Gino and Remy asked at the same time.

"Um, we met at the funeral," Cam mumbled. "Hey birthday boy, this is your other granny," she said, trying to lighten the mood.

"He looks just like my boys did at that age!"

"That's what Jean said," Cam smiled before looking at him. "Happy birthday, by the way."

He smiled. "Thanks. This is Remy, my godsister."

"Nice to meet you finally," Remy said. "Happy birthday, handsome."

Ian smiled, like he did with all women, and they laughed.

"He's such a flirt," Cam said. "Let me introduce you all to everybody."

They went into the living room and Cam introduced everyone. Everyone kind of looked shocked when Ian reached for Gino.

He put his gift down and grabbed him up quick, making him laugh with the faces he made.

"Wow," Mia whispered. "Like looking at a ghost."

Cam sighed before clapping her hands. "Let's get this party started!"

After everyone ate, Cam let Ian open a few of his gifts. He was sitting on the living room floor and Gino was next to him, making car noises and playing with him.

Remy watched silently, almost in shock of how well Gino adapted to fatherhood. She had been quiet most of the day, but that was because she didn't want to say the wrong thing and give him away. She knew that he was scared of losing Cam and Ian again, no matter how much he wouldn't admit it. Remy was determined to make sure Jean's death and all of Gino's schemes were not in vain.

Remy looked and saw Granny Watson about to get up with an empty plate but she stopped her.

"I got it, Ma."

"I want some more chicken, child," she said. Remy nodded.

"Got it."

Before she made it to the kitchen she heard raised voices, so Remy stopped and moved out of sight.

"What are they doing here?" Jayson asked.

"Excuse you?" Cam said. "What are you doing here?"

Jayson sighed. "Cam, you need to be careful. I'm just worried about you."

"Worried about me now? You dipped out, remember?"

"You're mad about me getting a better job, baby…"

Cam laughed. "Nope, don't do this."

Jayson sighed. "Can't we talk about it?"

"No!" Cam snapped. "It's my son's birthday. Nothing else deserves my attention," Cam said. When it got quiet, Remy knew one of them was about to walk out so she quickly walked in.

"Okay, Granny Watson," she said behind her before turning and stopping. "Oh, I'm sorry! Was I interrupting?"

"No," Cam said. "You need anything?"

Remy smiled slowly, noticing Jayson back up but not leave out. "Granny Watson wants more chicken…"

"Oh sure," Cam said, taking the plate from her. "My best friend's fiancé is a great cook, right?"

"He sure is," Remy said, her eyes still on Jayson. "You know Cam…Jean and Granny Watson are very excited about being able to get to know Ian. It means a lot."

Cam sighed. "It means a lot to me, too. I definitely want Ian to know all the family he has."

"Exactly."

Cam cleared her throat as she handed Remy the plate. Remy looked at both of them and smirked. She walked out and went to hand Granny Watson the plate again.

"What's up with her?" Jayson asked. Cam sighed.

"If you're going to be in here, at least help me clean up."

About an hour later, Ian began to get fussy, so Nana took him in the back for his nap. Jeremiah and Cam ended up playing dominoes against Remy and Gino.

"Mia can't play so I always gotta be his partner," Cam joked. They all laughed but Mia sucked her teeth.

"That's alright!"

"I'll teach you one day, baby," Jeremiah said, leaning over to kiss her. She pushed him a little and sat down on the couch. Jeremiah laughed hard and blew her a kiss.

"Mia and Jeremiah are getting married soon," Cam said.

Granny Watson clapped. "That's a blessing!"

"Thank you, ma'am," Mia said. "We haven't set a date yet."

"Remy, what about you?" Cam asked. "You got someone special."

"No."

Cam looked to see if she would talk more but she didn't. Gino slammed a domino down on the table and Remy cheered him on.

"Domino!" he said. "Wash them bones."

Remy and Gino ended up winning. It was getting late, so Cam started helping people pack to go plates with the left over food and cake. Remy sat back next to Gino, making sure no one was around before nodding towards Jayson.

"You know who this dude is?" she whispered.

"Mia's cousin..."

"That's all?" she asked. Gino glanced at her.

"What's up?"

"I think him and Cam had something going on."

Gino watched Jayson move for a minute, trying to figure out if he'd seen him before. While keeping tabs on Cam, he hadn't seen her around any man except for Jeremiah. As much as he wanted to believe she hadn't seen anyone over the last year, he wouldn't be stupid.

But that didn't mean he had to like it.

"What you hear?" Gino asked. Remy smirked and told him what she heard before she went into the kitchen. "Right."

"Be cool," Remy said. "I see that look in your eye."

"He came to my son's birthday party," Gino said, more to himself than Remy. His jaw flexed a little and Remy sighed before making him look at her.

"Hey! Chill out, bro. Now is not the time."

"Don't tell me what to do," he smirked, trying to relax back on the couch, but still keeping an eye on Jayson, who was now having a conversation with Nana.

"Yeah well, somebody has to," Remy said, rolling her eyes. "Don't mess up the plan because you jealous."

Gino smirked. "Territorial," he said. "There's a difference."

TEN

The next time Cam saw Jean, she had invited him to the park with her and Ian. She had to admit that ever since Ian's birthday, she had been feeling a little weird around him. She figured it was because he reminded her so much of Gino. Cam hadn't known any twins before, but she heard they were pretty in tune with each other.

Cam just noticed too many similarities in their personalities. Jean did little things that Gino used to do for her. It was all too familiar and Cam couldn't help but feel it in the gut of her belly. In her apartment, he seemed so comfortable. Cam felt that being outside in the open air would help settle those feelings.

"You want some ice cream?" Jean asked. Cam looked towards where he pointed to see the small ice cream stand near the back of the park. She nodded.

"Just a vanilla cone," she said. "Ian likes vanilla." Jean nodded before walking over to the cart. Cam busied herself getting a few of Ian's toys out that she brought with them. He had fallen asleep in the car, so it would take him a few minutes to figure out where they were.

Cam smiled down at him, finger combing his kinky, black hair. She was still contemplating getting his hair cut. Nana had been badgering her about it since he turned one, but it wasn't so unmanageable that she felt it needed to be cut.

"You ready to be a big boy, huh?" Cam asked. Ian ignored her and got busy with his toys. Cam laughed and played with him until Jean came back.

"Oh," she said in surprise, reaching for the cone. "How'd you know I like sprinkles?"

"…Who doesn't?" he asked. Cam laughed before licking the cone. She shivered a little from how he looked at her. "You okay?"

"Yeah…just caught a little chill."

He looked around before sitting next to her. "Been a long time since I been in some grass like this."

Cam laughed. "I do a lot of things I haven't done in forever now that I have a kid. I used to hate sand boxes! No telling what animals do in there. First time Ian wanted to go in one, I tried to clean the sand first."

He laughed. "You crazy!"

Cam looked at him in amusement. "What's so funny? I'm so serious right now!" she tried not to laugh.

"I know, that's what's funny."

They both laughed. Ian threw his toy in between them and mumbled something. Gino looked at him in shock and Cam laughed.

"He's a very spoiled baby."

"That won't be good when he's older," Gino warned. Cam shrugged.

"It's just me and him...I'm glad he wants my attention. When he's older he won't want nothing to do with me."

Gino watched them for a moment and sighed. "You're wrong about that."

Cam looked at him and frowned. "How you figure?"

Gino sighed, wanting to tell her how well she was doing at raising his son on her own. How she'd grown so much since they were together. He thought of an old Jaheim song about a diamond in the rough and couldn't help but relate it to her. All the stuff she'd gone through while she was pregnant, all the things him and Tameka put her through, hadn't stopped her from being the beautiful woman and mother she was.

It was hard not to love her. Even all the immature decisions she made and how naive she was at times didn't stop her spirit from shining through.

Gino didn't pray often, but he prayed every night now that when the time came for him to reveal himself to his love, she'd find some type of way to accept him... again.

He sighed, putting those thoughts aside as best as he could. "Just a feeling."

Cam huffed before tickling Ian. "We'll see, but for now him loves his mommy, huh?" Ian fell over on her laughing, trying to push her hands away. "Say I love mommy the most!"

Gino remained mostly quiet for the rest of the time, his feelings for Camryn becoming too strong for him to keep up his lie. He focused on Ian for a little while longer before he made up a lie about having to be somewhere. After making sure they were in the car and headed home, Gino quickly made his way back to his hotel to get his thoughts together.

Baby sighed as she picked up Gino's call. She knew he was probably upset that she hadn't answered the previous ones, but she honestly didn't know what to say.

"This how you treat the person who got you out of jail?" he asked. Baby rolled her eyes.

"Been busy, any news?" she asked, getting to the point.

"I sent someone to check it out."

Baby huffed. "Why not just give me the info and let me handle it? Why drag this out?"

"I know you anxious to get your hands on her, but we doing this my way."

"Typical," she mumbled.

"What was that?"

"What you want since you ain't gonna let me handle it now," Baby said. Gino laughed.

"I'll be in town in a couple days. Once I make sure all this pans out, I'll give you what you want."

Baby smiled and licked her lips. She could practically feel Tameka dying by her hands. She hadn't slept since she'd been out. It was easier to deal with Twan being gone when she was in jail. It was too much to worry about.

Now that she was home, Baby couldn't sleep in her bed without him. Twan made her feel like she was worth something. He valued her as his equal and knowing that Tameka tricked her into helping her set up Gino and still killed Twan was eating her alive.

"Good," she said, staring at the wall. "I saw Lori today."

"She say anything to you?" Gino asked. He half expected Lori to tell someone about their little encounter by now. Gino even thought Chase would come at him, but nothing had happened yet. He was half suspicious and half entertained by the fact that both of them ran their months when they felt he wouldn't do anything. Their talk was cheap; nothing had changed in that department.

"Nah, she ain't see me," Baby replied. "And I was handling business so I ain't have time to speak."

Gino sucked his teeth. "Don't go running around being obvious. If you need some money let me know, but I need you to lay low."

Baby rolled her eyes, not wanting anymore favors from Gino. "I'm good. Hit my line when it's time."

Baby hung up and turned her cell phone off before lying down and looking up at the ceiling of her bedroom. She had to figure out a plan to get out of that house. She was hurt that Twan's people weren't going to let her stay in his place. His mom never really liked her, but since they thought she was responsible for turning him against Gino, none of them would deal with her.

It was crazy how she was the one everyone was holding responsible for the downfall of Gino and Twan.

Twan's resentment for Gino started way long before Baby came around.

Baby couldn't stand the thought of helping Gino in anyway. He was lucky that her wanting Tameka dead was personal revenge that just happened to work out for the both of them.

Baby's eyes rolled when her bedroom door burst open and Keisha waltzed in.

"I need an outfit."

"Everything in here is mine," Baby said, still looking up at her ceiling.

Keisha snickered. "You ain't pay for it. Aunt Janetta been letting me borrow your stuff. Stop tripping."

"I'm home, so that ends now."

Keisha sucked her teeth. "Fine. Still stuck up I see."

"Keisha what you want? You always over here for what? Aunt Kayla barely talk to Momma."

"Excuse us for being there for your lonely momma while you were locked up for murder!" Keisha said. Baby slowly sat up on her bed and looked at Keisha with red in her eyes.

"You got a few seconds to apologize and watch your mouth."

Keisha sucked her teeth. "You ain't running nothing."

Baby smiled. For the first time since she'd been home, she felt like herself. The adrenaline that she always felt before a fight was a welcomed feeling that she accepted quickly.

Before Keisha could even blink, Baby had her pinned against the wall, kneeing her in her stomach. Keisha doubled over in pain and yelled for Janetta to come get Baby. Baby pulled her in before slamming her back against the wall.

"Shut up! You wanted this!" Baby yelled. "At least fight back."

"You're crazy!" Keisha said, trying to push her away. Baby pushed her against the dresser and Keisha groaned. Deciding not to go too hard on her, Baby leaned in and whispered in her ear.

"I'ma let you go and you are gonna move your ass out of my room and stay out of it," Baby said. "Don't make me repeat myself."

Keisha huffed. "Just let me go."

Baby held her there for a second before pushing her down on the carpet. Keisha took a second to catch her breath before stumbling out of Baby's room. She watched her for a moment before slamming her door shut and locking it.

Walking over to her vanity, Baby pulled her hair up into a messy bun on top of her head and looked over her skin to make sure Keisha's scratches hadn't done any damage. She smiled when she was satisfied with her reflection.

"I'm gonna tell her the truth."

Gino waited a minute to see if Granny Watson would respond.

"Okay."

He frowned. "Just okay? I thought that's what you wanted."

"Son, it really depends on what you're doing it for?"

"She deserves to know."

"Is that your only reason?"

Gino sighed. "Granny, what you trying to say?"

"Don't sass me," she said. "What's different now than a few weeks ago when I told you to tell her the truth in the first place?"

Gino thought about the last time he had seen Cam which in reality was only a few days, but felt like forever. The more comfortable he got around her and Ian, the more he wanted to truly be with his family. He could sense that Cam knew something was up and he couldn't risk losing her if she found out any other way.

He'd want her to know before everyone else so she could decide if she wanted to try again with him.

"What are you going to do if she doesn't accept you?" Granny Watson asked, not waiting for an answer for her previous question.

"I can't keep pretending," he whispered.

"I know it's hard," Granny Watson said. "But remember why you started this."

Hearing Jean's name all the time was weighing heavy on Gino. It didn't bother him as much when Baywood or Chase said it, but hearing Cam say it twisted at his heart. Jean was gone.

"I miss him," Gino admitted.

"I miss him, too," Granny Watson said. "Only one of y'all that never gave me much trouble." she teased. Gino smirked, knowing it was true. "You and yo momma were just so damn rowdy. Jean got his calmness from me."

Gino laughed. "Since when you been calm?"

"Hush child."

"I'm playing, Granny."

"…So now, answer my question. Why tell her now?"

Gino sighed, looking around at the hotel room while he decided that his time there was limited. "I want my family back."

A few days later, Gino showed up at Cam's door, ready to reveal himself to her. He would have come sooner, but he took his Granny's advice and took a few days to himself to get his thoughts together. He stayed at the hotel and turned his phone off. The only thing that time proved was that he was right to feel the way he felt.

Gino had no idea why God had given him a second chance at life, especially when he had been the reason so many ended in the past. His ignorance to that fact wouldn't stop him from living in the moment. Telling Cam the truth was his first act of redemption as Gino.

When the front door opened, Gino shook himself out of his own thoughts and smirked to see Cam standing in front of him. In that moment, he remembered the young 17-year-old girl he'd wait for after school all those years ago.

They'd been through a lot within the last four years. He was hoping their good times would help her accept their new reality a little easier.

"Hey Jean," Cam said, opening her apartment door with a small frown on her face. "Ian is actually with Mia for the night. If I would have known you were coming, I would have called you," she said.

He shook his head. "Nah, my bad for popping up, but I actually need to talk to you about something."

Camryn's frown did not lift, but she stepped aside to let him in. Shutting the door behind him, he quickly turned back towards her.

"Make sure you lock that."

Camryn laughed a little. "Gino always did that."

He cleared his throat. "...My bad."

"So, what's up? Everything okay?"

"...Can you sit down?"

Camryn kept her eyes on him as she walked over to her couch and slowly sat down. She had been getting weird vibes from him for the last couple of weeks, but tried not to think much of it, assuming he just reminded her too much of his twin. "What's going on?"

"Remember when we were talking before and I was telling you all the stuff G told me about you two?" Camryn nodded. "I left one thing out."

"What?"

"Do you remember the last night you saw him?"

Camryn's eyes immediately shut. She tried not to remember that night so many times, but it was the last time she saw him and the last time he actually revealed his true feelings. She opened her mouth to tell him that she did, but closed it before taking a moment to think. "Why?"

"You had that scare at Denny's and he took you to the hospital. He was so worried about the baby...worried that he had harmed him in some way."

Camryn shook her head as her throat began to burn. "I don't wanna talk about that."

"When he drove you back to the parking lot to get your car, do you remember what he told you?"

Camryn stood up and walked into the kitchen, but he followed her. "That's enough!"

"He told you that he lied about loving you," He said, trapping Camryn between the counter and his own body. She froze in fear and shock. "That he loved you and his son. You remember that?"

"Why...why would he tell you that?" she asked, breathing hard.

"...He didn't." Gino said, moving her hair from her face. Camryn's heart broke before shaking her head, reading between the lines of what he was saying.

"How do you know then?" she whispered slowly.

"You felt it right? Ever since that day at the park, you looked at me like you knew. I could tell that you could feel what we had and it scared you because you thought I was him. You thought you knew the truth."

Camryn immediately began to cry. "This isn't happening!"

"No matter what we went through, we had a connection Cam and that was why it was so easy for you to let me in. You were scared but you could tell how much I needed to be with you and my son."

Camryn tried to swallow to soothe her throat, but it was no use. "....Gi...Gino?"

"It's me, baby."

"...I watched them bury you....you were in the casket. Please get off of me! Why are you doing this?"

Camryn tried to move but Gino pulled her closer to his body and pressed his lips against her chin. "You watched them bury my brother. I wouldn't put you through this if it wasn't true, baby. What you need me to tell you to make you know it's me?"

Camryn's head began to pound and her vision got blurry. Her knees buckled but since he was holding her, she did not fall.

"I can't...this isn't..."

"Calm down, breathe, and tell me what you want me to do."

"...I need you to back up and give me some air."

Gino licked his lips and smirked, stepping back with his hands up in the air.

"Ask me anything."

"When did we meet?"

"You were walking home from school. Ask me something hard."

Camryn tried hard not to smile. "Okay, I got one. What happened the night before Nana came home from the hospital?"

Gino sighed. "You got sick while we were making love and that's when you found out you were pregnant a few days after."

Camryn exhaled deeply, trying to control her breathing. "I have one more question."

"Okay."

"How is this possible?"

"You want to sit?" he asked. Camryn shook her head no. "That night I told you I had gone home to visit and something wasn't right, you remember that?" Camryn nodded. "After I left you, I drove back home. I was going to give my granny and Jean all my info to my accounts because I knew something would go down. My granny was hysterical and Jean convinced me to let him go handle it, saying I was too preoccupied with what was going with me and you to think level headed."

"But why didn't I know you had a twin?" Camryn asked.

"No one did, not Tameka, not Twan...only my family back home. Jean had photophobia."

"What is that?"

"His eyes were real sensitive to light. He rarely left the house and if he did he had shades on."

Cam took a moment to think about it. "So he came back and got killed at the house," she finished. Gino nodded. "Even if I believed this...why wait months to come back? Won't you get in trouble for faking your own death?"

"I had to make sure my granny was okay and tried to figure out what happened before I went back. I knew Meka had something to do with it and it was more than just the story given at Baby's trial....and I didn't fake my death. The death certificate has Jean's name on it, only the funeral."

Camryn placed her hand over her chest and closed her eyes, trying to put everything together. She was confused and not sure if she believed him. However, part of her was relieved that she no longer had to feel guilty for feeling a certain way about Gino's twin. If it was truly him, then their

attraction was never lost, but she suddenly feared something else.

"So are you here to take him from me?" she asked.
Gino frowned before shaking his head violently.

"I'm here to take you both with me."

Camryn's eyes widened. "G...I can't just..."

"Hear me out," he said, throwing his arms up. "I just
want to be with my family. If you want to stay here cool,
but I have a house for us back home. Away from the drama.
It can be me, you, and our son. I'll spend the rest of my life
trying to undo what I did to you if you let me."

"I'm away from the drama here..." she mumbled. Camryn moved to get out of the kitchen. Gino sighed before
wrapping his arms around her and surprising her with a
very heated kiss. Camryn stumbled back but he kept her in
his arms and kissed her harder. Camryn lost control and
gave into the kiss. Any doubt that she had of that being
Gino was killed in that kiss. It felt like their whole relationship and all of her feelings came rushing back to her
through his lips, even the bad times. She began to cry as
she kissed him back, almost hating herself that she had
missed him so much.

"Why would you do this to me?" she cried as she
kissed him, groaning when he picked her up and began to
walk to her bedroom. Her heart pounded. Although her
body screamed at his touch, she hadn't been sexually involved in months. Once she and Jayson began to get rocky
a few months before he left, she vowed to be celibate.
Gino's large hands flattened against her shoulders and
pulled her into him. Camryn's eyes rolled back as she
moaned into their kiss and let him carry her over to her bed.

He didn't move to take her clothes off right away, but his body heat on top of hers made Camryn feel like she'd already been penetrated. Gino moved to pull her shirt over her head and Camryn finally came to her senses and pulled away from the kiss.

"What? What's wrong?" he breathed heavily. "You still don't believe me."

Camryn shook her head. "It's not that...I....this is too much right now."

Gino looked into her eyes for a moment and Camryn could see him physically trying to control his breathing. He pecked her lips once again before backing up and sitting next to her on the bed.

"Okay," he said softly, running his hand down his face and taking a few deep breaths. Camryn sat stunned, staring at him. He looked over at her and smirked. "What?"

"Are you sure you aren't the other twin?" she asked. Gino laughed hard for the first time in a while before pulling Camryn's into his side and lying back on the bed with her.

"Some things changed," he said.

"I see," she mumbled. Her head was still swarming with questions but she snuggled close to him and pushed her face into his neck. Camryn would get to the bottom of everything going on but right now she was just relieved that she hadn't been developing feelings for her son's uncle like she thought she was.

For the rest of the night, the two lay in bed together, talking about everything and nothing. Gino asked her what she had been doing since she moved and what her job was like. He asked if she had been dating and she told him she had, but didn't go into detail about it.

"You getting by?" he asked.

"Yeah," she said. "We're good."

Gino nodded. "I been wanting to ask you to make me some spaghetti for weeks."

Cam laughed. "What made you wait so long to reveal the truth?"

Gino looked at her before pressing his hand to her back and bringing her closer to him.

"I had everything planned out, except for this."

"I don't understand."

"I didn't know how I'd find you. The only thing I had to go off was you mentioning Mia's school a while back. I had an idea of what I would say when I saw you, but…"

"But what?" Cam asked, rubbing his head like she used to in order to relax his mind or calm his nerves. Gino closed his eyes for a moment and enjoyed it. "But what?"

"When I saw my son…my mind went blank."

Cam thought of something. "So Mikel wasn't your brother's name?"

"It was Jean's middle name."

Cam smiled. "That worked out…is that why you told me your little brother died when you were younger?"

Gino nodded. "It was just easier not to explain him. Didn't want anyone to try and hurt them…"

"I understand…I think."

Cam watched him and smiled, still in awe of what was going on. She began to think about everything they went through and she sighed.

"Why'd you marry her?" Cam asked, suddenly. Gino stopped laughing and ran his hand down his face. "I can't figured it out at all."

"I owed it to her."

Cam waited to see if he would elaborate. "Explain?"

Gino sighed. "I ran her life. She did all I wanted for so long and I was never faithful to her. Before you, it was just random women."

"Why was I different?" Cam whispered.

"You know why," Gino whispered.

"...So what are you going to do when you find her?" Cam asked.

"...Call Mia and tell her to bring Ian home."

Cam sighed before nodding. She reached for her phone but stopped when she thought about Mia.

"How am I going to tell her this?" Cam thought. Mia was never a fan of Gino and Cam could bet all the money in the world that Mia would be against Cam even talking to him right now.

"How about I just get him in the morning," Cam said, turning back around. "We still have some catching up to do."

Gino nodded before pulling Cam back to his side. The silence became a little overwhelming, so Cam turned on her radio and let whatever song she was listening to before play.

Gino hadn't felt this peaceful in months. Lying there with Cam made him feel like all the planning and scheming he'd done was worth it.

He began to think back on the last couple of years dealing with Cam. He knew that it would take some time for her to trust him again, but the fact that she was willing allowed him to breathe a little easier.

He had never really done right by her, not entirely. When they first started out, he kept her looking nice, helped with bills and loved her down as much as she could stand. Given their circumstances, they were good until she got pregnant.

Gino shuddered at the thought of Twan following his orders to force Cam to miscarry.

Feeling him tense up, Cam turned to look up at him and frowned. "What's wrong?"

Gino sat up and scratched his head. "Sit up for me."

Cam used her elbows to slowly elevate herself to where she could sit up.

"I guess we aren't done talking."

"We need to talk about the night Twan came to your house."

Cam's eyes darkened. "You mean the night you sent him to kill my child."

Gino sighed. "Cam, I…"

"You what?" she asked, cutting him off. "Why are we even talking about this?"

"I'm trying to apologize to you."

"I don't want it."

Gino frowned. "What?"

"I don't want to hear why you thought you were doing the right thing."

Gino sighed as Cam got up from the bed and began to pace the carpet.

"Just let me explain myself."

"You have no idea how it felt to wake up thinking my baby was gone!" Gino frowned, not at her emotion but how quickly it came out. "Then having to hide in fear most of my pregnancy because you weren't man enough to take responsibility for what we did."

"I know all of that, baby."

"Do you? Because it seems as if you think you're God."

"I used to," he said. That shut Cam up. "I was invincible in my mind and everybody knew it. I ran everything around me and up until you got pregnant you were no exception."

"Get out," Cam said. Gino stood up and walked over to her with his hands up in surrender.

"Listen to what I'm saying. All that is different now. Why do you think I'd let me brother come back instead of me?" Cam shook her head. "Exactly! None of this makes sense. I handled everything, I called the shots. I can't even comprehend what I was thinking when I went along with his plan. I can't explain how you didn't miscarry and I can't explain how I'm not dead."

"Why are you telling me this?" Cam mumbled, folding her arms across her chest to hug herself.

"There's a lot I don't get," he said softly. "But one thing I am damn sure of is that you loved me. You didn't love me because of my money. You loved the me that was with you and I wouldn't admit it then but I loved that, too."

Cam began to cry. "Why did it have to go this far?"

"I'm sorry," he said, pulling her into a hug. "Let me fix it."

"You can't fix the past," she mumbled into his shirt.

Gino thought about the rest of his plan and how he wanted to avenge his brother's death. He was sure Cam wouldn't be down with the plan, but he knew he couldn't move on in life knowing that the person responsible for his twin's death was still walking around, pretending to have a little pretty life. Once he got rid of Tameka, he could focus on his family.

"…I'm gonna try my best to."

ELEVEN

"You can't beat me boy!" Gino yelled. Ian went into a fit of laugher as he fell against him on the kitchen floor. Cam smiled. Even with her back to them while she cooked breakfast, she couldn't help but be giddy about the growing relationship.

It had only been four days since Gino's big reveal and nothing about his interactions with Ian changed. They still wrestled and watched television together and everything he had been doing since he came into their lives again.

Now that Cam knew for sure that Gino was who he was, it warmed her heart that Ian had his father. She had been so happy that even Mia's hesitation hadn't ruined it for her. Nana was behind her decision to let Ian know that Gino was his father; she just wanted her to be careful.

The night after Gino revealed who he truly was, Cam told Mia. Mia was upset that Cam believe it or even let him back in the house. Cam knew Mia still didn't believe the story, but that wasn't her concern right now. Mia was living her life and Cam would have to live hers.

"You sure you only want two pancakes?" Cam asked.

"Yeah," Gino said before making car noises with the tiny car in his hand. Ian clapped his hands before reaching for another car that sat in front of them. They played that way until Cam announced that breakfast was ready.

They ate in silence, unless either of them interacted with Ian.

"You sure you want to go back?" she asked.

"Gotta put the house on the market," Gino said. "You don't have to come."

"No, it's okay. Nana rented the house out so I can go check on it," Cam said. Gino looked at her for a second and then nodded. He didn't think it was dangerous for Cam to go back with him, he just didn't want her to think about all the bad things that happened there when he was trying to keep her focused on the good.

He also planned on revealing himself to Baywood and Chase. He wanted to see if Chase still talked as much as he had been thinking Gino was his twin.

The only other part of his plan was underway with little supervision from him.

While Cam cleaned up, he made a call to Remy to let her know that her train ticket was waiting. He needed her help with the house and he wanted her to keep an eye on Cam and Ian while he handled business. She was more than willing to make the trip.

"I'll admit, I'm a little excited," Cam said. Gino smirked before pulling her into his arms. "I haven't been home since before I had Ian. May stop by and see Mia's mom. She's only seen him once when he was only a few months old."

"That sounds like a good idea," Gino said, thinking if Cam stayed busy it would make the trip go smoother and quicker.

"Feels like forever," Cam said. She sighed as she looked around trying to figure out why her hometown felt so unfamiliar. It hadn't even been that long since she'd been there, but everything about it felt different. Gino rubbed her thigh as he gave her a soft glance.

"I was just thinking that," he said. Cam bit her lip before looking into the backseat of the truck. Ian was still sleep, which meant he would be hell on legs around bedtime. Cam giggled, thinking she'd let Gino handle that. "What?"

"Nothing, what hotel are we at?"

"Hilton."

"Near the freeway exit?" she asked. Gino nodded while he continued to drive. Cam sent Mia's mom a text and let her know that she'd be to see her later that evening. "You staying with us for a second when we get there?"

"Nah, the realtor is waiting on me," he said. Cam could feel that it was more to this visit than the house, but she nodded her head anyway.

"You be good for Momma while I'm gone," Gino said to Ian as he put him down on the carpet in the hotel room. Ian ran off to explore and Cam smiled. Ever since the reveal, Gino had been saying that to Ian. Cam thought it

159

was cute, even though she never had any real issues with Ian's behavior thus far since he was only one.

"What time will you be back?" Cam asked, sliding her hands over his shoulders and around his neck. Gino secured her in his arms before shrugging his shoulders. "What about dinner?"

"Just order room service if you want."

"…Okay."

Gino lifted her chin so he could look into her eyes. "What's wrong?"

"Nothing," she said, trying to move away from him. He shook his head and held her still.

"You know better."

"We just…haven't eaten apart as a family since…" she trailed off, knowing that her point had been made. Gino studied the solemn look on her face and fought hard internally on not smiling in amusement.

"You're cute," he said. Cam sucked her teeth before pushing him away. "I'll be back. Call me before you order."

Cam smiled as he closed the hotel room door behind him.

As if a switch went off in his brain, Gino went back into business mode as soon as he walked out of the hotel's main entrance. He couldn't help but be frustrated that he wasn't able to find Tameka yet.

He called Remy for the third time that day.

"I'm headed to the train station now," she said. "I can't believe this bitch."

"You think she did it on purpose?" he asked. He never thought Lori was smart, but she couldn't have been dumb enough to give them a fake address.

"It don't matter at this point," she said. "I'll handle her. You just need to think of somewhere she might be. We back to square one at this point."

Remy had gone to keep an eye on Tameka until Gino was ready to deal with her a few days ago. He wanted to get a feel for her habits and see when the best possible time to strike was, but when Remy called him and said Tameka was no where in sight, they knew that Lori had played them.

Now he had two bombs to drop: him being Gino and Lori getting pregnant by Moe. He had no idea how he was going to find Tameka, but since Lori wanted to be cute and keep playing, Gino had no problem with airing her dirt out.

"Alright, I'll be to get you when the train gets here."

"Cool."

Gino hung up and headed to Baywood's place. It was late in the afternoon and Baywood liked to do all his errands early, so he knew he'd be home. Gino smirked as he thought about how smooth Baywood had things running now. It would be easy for him to get back in, if that was his life now. He knew Cam would never go for it and he was honestly tired of it anyway.

He didn't want to ruin his second chance.

Gino called Baywood once he made it to the block.

"What's up, Jean?"

"I need to holla at you," he said.

"Go head."

"Nah," he said. "I'm back in town. Where you at?"

"…Around. What's up?"

Gino sucked his teeth. "Meet me at Twan's old house." He hung up before Baywood could protest. Gino took the next left and felt his blood boil a little as he neared his former best friend's old home. Twan had moved out of it when him and Baby got serious, but Gino knew the house remained unoccupied.

It only took him about five minutes to get there. He got out and leaned against the truck before lighting the blunt he had. Gino thought of all the times he'd spent there once he moved into the city. He always acted tough, but he missed home and being around Twan made him feel like he had family. They built an empire together and Gino still couldn't figure out why Twan got greedy. Baby filling his head was one thing, but Gino felt it had to be deeper than that.

He shook his head, remembering how Twan got off on Gino being confused on his situation with Camryn. Even after Twan thought he'd killed their baby, he seemed to take pleasure in the fact that Gino had second thoughts. He should have saw it then.

Baywood's car pulled up slowly in front of the truck. Gino looked up at the sky and blew a puff of smoke. Once he heard the car door close it was only a few seconds before Baywood was in front of me.

"What's up? What's so urgent? You find Meka?"

Gino looked at him and shook his head. "I'm Gino." Baywood just looked at him with a blank stare. "I'm Gino."

"I heard you the first time," Baywood said. "Doesn't make it true."

Gino laughed. "Remember when you and your ol lady first started kicking it and she found out you were trapping? She ran up on the spot downtown and I pulled a gun out on her. You was spazzing out and pulled a gun on me. You the only person ever did that, that's still alive."

"You know a story," Baywood said. "Good for you."

"I know the combo to the safe house on 5th was your seeds expected delivery date before I left. I know we changed it every 90 days to keep niggas on they toes. I know you were the one who told me something was going down when Twan started stealing. Want me to keep going?"

"Nah nigga!" Baywood said. "Get to the part to where you died and we found out you had a twin!"

Gino sighed, telling Baywood the same story he told Cam a few days ago.

"This ain't real life, man," Baywood said, backing up and pacing the sidewalk a little.

"You ever see a body when Meka called you to the house?"

Baywood shook his head. "Nah…"

"You see a body at the funeral?" Gino asked. Baywood blinked a few times before shaking his head no.

"There was no body?" he asked. Gino sighed and looked down at his feet.

"Nah, there was a body…"

Baywood sighed. "Man, even if I believed you. What you come back for?"

"Even if you believed me?" Gino asked, laughing. "What else you want?"

"A DNA test, nigga!" Baywood said, laughing beside himself and the situation. "Why you ain't tell me when you first got back?"

Gino sighed. "I don't trust Chase."

"Come on, man…"

"Straight up," Gino said. "Lori knows more than she letting on and I'on know if he know, but he protecting her."

"He supposed to, G," Baywood said. Gino looked up at his friend and smirked. "So what's your plan? Why tell me now?"

Gino smiled slowly, a sinister smile that Baywood was all too familiar with. "That's the question you need to be asking."

"Aw, Camryn, he's so handsome!"

Cam laughed as Ian giggled while Mia's mother, Miss Kathy, kissed his cheeks and tickled him.

"Thank you," she said. "Nana says she favors my mom, but I think he looks just like his dad."

Miss Kathy looked up at the mention of Gino but quickly looked back at Ian.

"I can see your mom a little."

"I take it Mia told you about his dad," Cam said. Miss Kathy sighed, but nodded. "So?"

Miss Kathy had been like a mom to Camryn ever since her and Mia became close in school. There were certain things that Nana was too tired to do and Miss Kathy never treated Cam any different then Mia when she was around.

"I don't really know much baby," she said. "But I learned a long time ago to stay out of the way of love."

Cam sighed, seeing she wasn't going to get any advice from Miss Kathy. "Understood."

"You hungry? I can make dinner. Invite him over so I can talk to him," Miss Kathy said.

"Momma Kathy, you don't need to cook for us," Cam said, rocking Ian on her lap.

"I know I don't," she said. "It'll be done by the time little man wakes up from his nap."

Cam looked down and smiled to see Ian was finally sleep. It seemed as if ever since Gino came back into their lives, he rarely took naps. "Well, at least let me help."

"You call that man of yours and let him know the plan."

Cam sighed. "You sure? I mean, I know you've known me all my life...but Jayson's your nephew."

"Let me tell you something," Kathy said, cutting Cam off. "I love my family, but if I would have had the chance to keep my family together, there would have been no questions about it." Cam looked down at Ian and nodded. "Your mom felt the same way about your dad."

Her eyes lit up. "Really? She never talked about him with me."

Kathy sighed. "She was heartbroken. Once he went to jail and your Nana moved you guys here, she wanted to forget him so it wouldn't hurt so much."

"She said Nana wouldn't even let her accept his letters."

"With your mom being so young, your Nana thought she was doing what was best for you both. That's all you can do when it comes to your child. You'll do what you think is best for you and that handsome little boy."

Cam smiled. "Thank you."

"Don't mention it," Kathy said. "Now stop distracting me from dinner."

Cam carefully laid Ian down next to her before pulling her phone out. She sent Mia a text, teasing her about the meal Miss Kathy was cooking before calling Gino. She smiled as he answered on the second ring.

"You good?" he asked.

"Yes, Mia's mom is cooking us dinner. You remember where she stays?"

"Yeah, but I have to pick Remy up from the train station. Would it be enough?"

Cam frowned, wondering why Remy was coming but decided against voicing her concerns. "Let me ask."

"We can just eat out."

"That's rude," Cam said before moving the phone. "Ma, is it enough for Gino's godsister?"

"Sure," Kathy said from the kitchen.

"Problem solved," Cam said back into the phone.

"You calling shots now, huh?" Gino teased. "You must have forgot who I am."

The deep octave in his voice made Cam obvious to the fact that he meant that in a sexual way. She clinched her thighs together and bit her lip. "Don't get quiet now."

"Shut up," Cam whined. "What are you doing? I miss you."

"How much?"

"Gino!"

He laughed. "I had to meet Baywood then we ran into some old friends. I'll be there soon, baby."

Cam blushed. "Okay, be safe."

Gino looked at Cam and Ian's picture on his phone for a moment after he hung up.

Baby sucked her teeth. "You done caking?" Baywood laughed.

"Would it matter?" Gino asked. "Unless you got something to tell me."

"My cousin at the daycare said the kids been there all week, so she ain't left town," Baby said. "We gotta find Tameka before she figures this shit out."

"It won't matter if she does or not," Gino said.

"Yeah, but it'll ruin the element of surprise," Baywood said.

Gino smirked. "Well, it's time to pay Chase and Lori a visit."

Baywood sighed. "Let's see what he knows first."

Gino rolled his eyes. "Get him to the house. I got a stop to make first."

Baywood nodded before getting out of the truck. Baby moved to get in the front, but Gino stopped her. "We gotta pick somebody up."

"I ain't sign up to be riding around with you."

"Tati, you got somewhere else to be? Or you done trying to get revenge for Twan's death?"

Her nose flared. "You don't care that he's dead anyway."

Gino turned around quick and grabbed her neck. "Watch your mouth! That was my brother. It would have never been handled that way if it was me. You lucky I don't buss your head open for putting him up to that shit in the first place! The only reason you breathing is out of respect for him."

Baby's eyes watered as she looked at him straight in his eyes and pushed him off of her. "Fuck you, Gino."

He turned around and started the truck. "Glad we cleared that up."

No more than 30 minutes later, Gino pulled up at the train station.

"What is she here for?" Baby asked.

"To help you find Meka."

"I don't need help."

"Obviously you do!" Baby sucked her teeth, but didn't respond. "Here she comes so shut up."

Remy jumped in the front seat and immediately turned around to look at Baby. "You talking shit?"

"Excuse you?"

"These windows ain't tinted, boo. Got something you want to say to me while you in here rolling your neck?"

Baby rolled her eyes as Gino began to drive. "I'on even know you."

"Cool we'll let's keep it classy and get this shit done."

Baby wanted to smirk, knowing that was something she would say, but didn't want to give Remy the satisfaction.

"What's the plan? Where fam at?"

"Chilling," Gino said. "We gotta go check this nigga Chase." Baywood sent Gino a message saying Chase's car was at home but he wasn't answer his phone. Gino wanted to respect Baywood, but he knew what he had to do.

"Finally!" Remy said. "Can't wait to burst this bitch's bubble."

"Who Lori? What's up?" Baby asked.

Remy smiled. "You'll see."

Lori tried her best to control her breathing as she tried to hear what Chase and Baywood were whispering about. She had been trying to call Tameka, but she never answered. Lori hadn't heard anything from Jean in the last few weeks, but something told her that this was far from over.

She heard car doors close outside, so Lori looked out the window to see who it was.

"Baby, someone's outside," Lori said, walking into the living room. "And we need to go pick the twins up."

"Alright, chill fat momma," he said, kissing her belly. "You speak to Wood?"

"Hey Baywood, you hungry?"

"Nah, I won't be long, just needed to scream at your man."

The doorbell rang.

"Bae, let them in."

Lori walked to the door and when she opened it, she nearly had a heart attack.

"Hey Lori!" Remy said. "Gonna let us in?"

"Why?" Lori whispered. Chase called her name and she sighed, moving aside to let them in.

"How is she out of jail?" Chase asked.

Baby sucked her teeth as she sat down and crossed her legs. "Hi to you, too."

Baywood sighed. "Bro, it's some crazy shit going on that we ain't know about."

"This again?" Chase snapped. "Gino gone, bro! Deal with it. Niggas die every day."

Gino smirked and shook his head. "Gino ain't dead, though."

"What?"

"I'm not dead," Gino said.

Chase looked around at everyone and laughed.

"So what? You show up and want the life your brother had so now you want to be him? Newsflash! He wasn't all that."

"Nigga, you been talking mad shit about how I was since I showed up. You ain't get enough last time you tried to run it?"

"You need to get out my crib, yo!"

Gino ignored his request. "You wasn't eating? I ain't take care of your shorties and hoe ass baby momma good enough while you was locked up?"

Everyone jumped up and Lori held her mouth and sat down when Chase pulled his gun out and pointed it at Gino.

"All this talking you doing don't phase me, but don't disrespect my chick again."

Gino smirked. "That bitch been in my business for years. The only reason I ain't pop her off was because of her loyalty to you and Tameka, but it seems like she's more loyal to Meka than you."

"She don't know shit!" Chase said. Lori started crying.

"Bullshit!" Remy yelled. "Tameka been calling her!"

"What? That don't mean I know where she is!" Lori cried.

"Guess again," Remy said. "Tell us where she is or your little secret gets aired out right now!" Remy said, holding up a small recorder. Lori's eyes grew wide.

"No, please. I told you what I know!"

"What the hell is going on?" Chase asked Lori, but she just cried. Baby sighed, leaning over towards Lori.

"Look, it's obvious you don't want want her to hit play, but she ain't bluffing. Is Meka really worth all this? Has she even looked back after framing me? She don't care about you! Otherwise she wouldn't have put you in this position."

Lori sobbed and put her head down. "I told her what I know," she mumbled, knowing what was about to happen.

Remy sucked her teeth before hitting play. Everyone got quiet to hear the recording as Lori kept crying.

"Why'd you tell her about the baby?" Lori asked.

"Hell, she was talking like she knew!"

"Who is that? Chase yelled. "Moe?"

"Keep listening," Remy said, Lori tried to get up and leave the room, but Chase grabbed her arm and pulled her to his side.

"I don't know how she figured it out."

"I ain't okay with this shit. You ain't even talked to me since you lost our baby," Moe said. Lori cried harder as Chase looked down at her with hurt and confusion in his eyes.

"Moe, we ain't doing this!" Lori snapped. *"Just don't say shit else to that bitch."*

"But what if.."

"I handled it."

Remy stopped the recording.

"Baby, let me explain," Lori started.

"Shut the hell up!" he yelled. "Put your shoes on."

She frowned. "Why?"

"You know why," Chase huffed.

"Well, our work here is done," Remy said.

"Nah," Chase said. "We all going to pay Moe a visit." He eyed Gino.

"Fine by me."

"Gino," Remy said, frowning. He looked at her confused for a moment before he sighed.

"As much as I'd love to see this, I got somewhere to be."

Baywood sighed. "I'll ride."

"Me too," Baby said.

Gino wasn't sold on the plan, but he knew he couldn't miss dinner, not if he wanted Cam to believe he had truly changed.

"Call me if you need me."

Lori all but held her breath in the front seat of Chase's car as he drove to Moe's house. He had seemed to calm down a little, which scared her even more.

"How in the hell did she get that recording?" Lori asked herself. She tried her best to remain calm for the baby's sake, but Lori knew someone was about to die. She just didn't know if it would be her, Moe or both of them.

"It's too early for them to deliver the baby if you kill me."

"Shut your stupid ass up," Chase said. Baby snickered in the backseat.

"Bro, is all this necessary?" Baywood asked.

"You'd let a nigga slide for knocking up your woman?" Chase asked. Baywood didn't respond. "Right."

Lori sighed. "I haven't touched him since you been home. I swear!"

"Don't change the fact that you let me mourn the death of another dude's kid. You would let me raise his baby?" He asked, finally looking at her. Lori's heart broke seeing the fire in his eyes. "If you ain't lose it? Was that your plan?"

Lori just cried and apologized over and over. She prayed Moe wasn't home when they got there. Even though she wasn't involved with him anymore, he helped her a lot while Chase was locked up. She tried not to get serious with him, but he was so sweet to her and the twins.

"You crying over this nigga?" Chase snapped. Lori shook her head violently.

"No," she lied. "I just…I don't know what you want me to do."

Baby laughed. "Probably not get pregnant by another dude."

"Would you shut up!" Lori snapped.

"Everybody shut up!" Chase said. Everyone got quiet when he pulled up in front of Moe's house. Lori sighed and closed her eyes, wishing she hadn't seen Moe's car in the driveway.

"What's up? You doing this or what?" Baywood asked.

Chase, who was breathing heavily, unlocked the door. "Go knock on the door."

Lori frowned. "What?"

"You heard what the fuck I said, Lori! Go tell that nigga to come outside and face me like a man!"

Lori's heart was beating out of her chest and it seemed as if the baby was as active as he'd ever been in that moment. She tried to calm him by placing one hand on her belly as she opened the door with her other. Lori turned around before she got out.

"Please, don't make me do this," she begged. Chase just glared at her. "I'm not trying to defend him or anything but I'm just as much to blame as him. Chase you were gone and the twins were out of hand and I was struggling. He didn't try and disrespect you, he was just helping out at first. I kind of approached him…"

She saw fire in his eyes and threw her hands up.

"You not helping," Chase said.

"I know baby, I'm just...I don't want you to go back to jail."

Chase snapped. "You don't want me to go back to jail? You sure? Maybe you was waiting on me to do something to go back so you could be with his nigga, huh? You mad you got pregnant by me again? Huh?"

Lori frowned. "What? No!"

"You wish I was still in jail to let this dude raise my kids?"

"No!" Lori yelled. "I don't want him! I was relieved when I lost the baby! I had no idea what was going on and he was trying to get me to leave you but I didn't want to! The only reason I even protected him was so you wouldn't go back to jail and leave me again! I didn't want his baby!"

Everyone got quiet as Lori looked at Chase to see what his next move was. She frowned when she saw him smile but her heart dropped when she heard someone behind her.

"Damn," Moe said. "And here I thought you was real, shawty."

Lori turned around slowly and sighed. "Moe, I'm sorry..."

Before Lori could finish her sentence, she heard a click behind her. Before she could turn to stop Chase, she jumped and screamed as a loud boom sounded. She felt the fire from the bullet brush past her head before Moe groaned and fell to the ground.

Lori was shaking as she grabbed her ear and felt blood coming from it. "I'm bleeding!" she yelled. Chase ignored her, jumped out the car, ran around to where Moe fell at and shot him two more times. He got back in the car and drove off. No one said anything except for Lori who was still crying.

Baby laughed as she recalled the story to Remy on what happened the night before.

"She was crying so hard like, 'no Chase baby, don't kill me,'" Baby said, shaking her head. "She's so pathetic."

Remy held her stomach and laughed. "Man, I would have paid to see her face," she said, pulling her hair up in a ponytail. "Would have been so much better than my night."

"What happened?"

Remy looked at her and sucked her teeth. "Not like you care."

Baby rolled her eyes. She hadn't known how she ended up in Remy's room at the hotel, but she thought they were getting cool, considering the situation. Baby never really had female friends and she didn't like the idea that she needed Remy's help. However, the way Remy handled herself was very similar to how Baby did.

"My bad," Baby said, rolling her eyes. "Thought we were bonding."

Remy looked at her and laughed. "Bonding? We in high school?"

Baby rolled her eyes. Remy sighed and sat down on the couch across from her. "I can go and you can sit in here lonely while G runs around with his boo."

Remy cut her eyes at her. "Fine," she said. Baby smirked. "He's different with her."

"Always was," Baby said. Remy frowned.

"How was that?"

Baby looked around the room, trying to figure out how to explain it. "Gino was ruthless, he didn't care about much and rarely showed any emotion outside of anger, but with her it was always a different type of anger."

"What you mean?" Baby asked.

"Meka went off her rocker when she found out that girl was pregnant. Tried to run her off the road and a whole bunch of mess," Baby said. "He almost killed Meka one day when he found out what she had been plotting."

"Well, I'm not surprised," Remy said. "But watching how he acts with her is like watching a whole different person. Like he changes just for her." Remy sighed. "I just don't want him to do all this because he feels bad."

"Well, he should feel bad," Baby said. "That girl didn't ask for all that. She got dragged in because she loved him!"

Remy eyed her. "I got a feeling you ain't just talking about her."

Baby fought back her emotions and shook her head. "I just get it, I guess."

Remy nodded. "He's in love though. Never seen him that way. He has a whole family now."

Baby nodded, realizing that Remy may have been feeling a little left out. They had both lost someone and everyone was just trying to figure things out. Baby still wasn't Gino's friend, but maybe Remy would be a different story.

"Let's go get a drink," Baby said. Remy's eyes lit up.

"Always down for that."

A few hours later, Baby and Remy were taking shots at a local bar. Men were buying them drinks and they were just laughing and flirting with them all.

"You didn't have to call him ugly!" Remy said. Baby rolled her eyes.

"I don't lie," she said with a straight face. They looked at each other and laughed before pushing their shot glasses together and taking their fourth shots.

"Oh, I needed this," Remy, shaking her head. "I'ma be sick…but I need it."

Baby laughed, holding up her glass before taking a sip. "You need a chaser."

"Tati, you are chasing liquor with liquor!"

"….Right."

Remy shook her head and laughed. She noticed the somber look on Baby's face.

"What?" Remy asked.

"Huh?"

Remy eyed her. "Why you looking like that?"

Remy turned to see what had Baby's attention, but there weren't many people in the bar. Remy saw a short, skinny woman leaning against the counter where the food orders were being taken. She had long braids that were blonde at the end and Remy could see the bright yellow on her nails from afar. She frowned and turned back to Baby.

"Who is that? You know her?"

"…Nah, thought I did though."

Remy nodded. "Well, let's take another shot!"

TWELVE

Cam frowned when she woke up and tried to move. Something was weighing her down and she almost yelled until she looked down and saw the arms holding her. She closed her eyes and smiled.

"No," Gino said. "Go back to sleep."

Cam giggled before turning around to face him. She sighed, running her hand along his jaw, still trying to process that the last couple of weeks hadn't been a dream.

"I'm real baby," he said with his eyes closed. Cam sucked her teeth and hit him in his arm. Gino caught her hand and kissed it before pulling her closer to him.

"Don't get comfortable," she said. "Your son will be up soon."

"Well, I'll get comfortable until then."

Gino kissed her neck and she sighed, relaxing into his embrace.

It was nearly March and the weather was beginning to break. Ever since they'd been back from selling the house, Gino hadn't left. Cam was concerned after a while about how he was living, but he assured her that he'd left the drug game alone. He had invested some money in flipping houses and currently had two rental properties: one that was occupied and one that he planned to move his family into.

Gino opened his eyes and looked at Cam as she groaned. Her neighbor was up and moving around loudly.

"She's so inconsiderate."

"Your house back home so far from neighbors, you ain't gotta worry about it," he said, rubbing her sides. Cam rolled her eyes playfully. "Yard big enough for Ian to play in."

"Aw yeah," she said. Gino nodded. "Who said I wanted a house?"

"You did," he said, matter-of-factly. "You were 19 I think, when that house make over show was all you used to watch."

"You remember that?" Cam asked. Gino bit his lip and nodded. Cam sighed, leaning in to kiss him just as she heard Ian begin to fuss. "Wanna get your son?"

"You love saying that when your ass wanna be lazy," he said. Cam laughed as he pushed the covers back and got out the bed.

Baby tapped her foot against the sidewalk outside of the middle school as she looked at her phone to check the time. She rolled her eyes as she realized she came too early, not really knowing what time school let out.

She was anxious. It had been weeks since she realized how she was going to find Tameka, but she hadn't been able to act on her plan until he was sure Gino and Remy were back out of town.

The bell rung and Baby slowly smiled, but didn't move. She kept her eyes on the door, waiting for one particular person. She pushed herself off the fence when she saw her.

"Hey Tani!"

Tani jumped a little at the sound of her name and looked around. When she saw Baby, her eyes widened for a second but then she shook her head and kept walking.

"Hey."

"How you been?" Baby said, walking fast to catch up with her.

Tani sighed. "What do you want, Baby?"

Baby pushed both her fists into the pockets of her hoodie and sucked her teeth.

"Where is Tameka?"

Tani looked at Baby and laughed. "Bitch, I knew you were crazy but I didn't know you were delusional."

Baby rolled her eyes. "Right."

"I'm serious! You think I'd tell you where my cousin is? Hell, I'm sure you mad she told on you. How you even get out of jail anyway?"

Baby clicked the gun in her pocket and she was sure Tani heard it because she stopped walking.

"Why don't you walk to my car and I'll tell you all about it."

Tani began to breathe heavily. She looked around to see if anyone was watching.

"Really?"

"Tani, don't test me! All these kids out here and your co-workers, too? You wanna get shot in front of them? I don't care about killing you."

"I'll tell you where she is, but you can't…"

"Nah, we going to do this my way. I gave you a chance, now I got other plans for you," Baby said, grabbing her arm. "Now walk."

Lori had been moving around the house as quietly as possible. It had only been a few days since Chase killed Mo, but she was sure he was still mad at her. Lori held her belly and sighed, knowing that her kids were probably the only reason she was still alive.

She had kept the twins out of daycare the last few days just so they'd be in the house.

"Take them to daycare tomorrow."

Lori jumped at the sound of Chase's voice behind her. She turned around and sighed.

"Um…their teacher…she's sick."

"Stop lying."

Lori sighed. "Chase, I…"

"Take them to daycare tomorrow."

She got up when he walked out the room and followed him. "Are you gonna talk to me at all?"

"You don't want me to talk to you," Chase said. "You really don't."

Lori bit her lip. "I can't deal with you walking around not talking to me."

Chase turned around and looked at her. "Aight, sit down and let's talk."

Lori backed up and looked at him as he sat down on the couch.

"I ain't mean like that," Lori mumbled.

"Oh yeah you did," Chase said with a sinister grin. "Sit your ass down."

Lori tried to clear her throat as she sat down on the couch opposite him. "I need to tell you what happened with me and Moe." Chase's nose flared, but he remained quiet. "I thought….the last time your appeal didn't go through that I'd be a single mom forever. Tameka was so caught up in Gino and I couldn't stand to see how she was acting, so I tried to keep my distance. Moe's aunt used to work at the twin's old daycare and he was around. Tia liked him and I was just lonely and at first we were just playing around."

"I don't wanna hear anymore," Chase said. Lori sighed, but nodded.

"I didn't mean for it to go that far," she whispered.

"So what did you mean? You keep saying that shit but you still ain't explained to me how you was gonna let me take care of this dude's baby?"

"Chase, I didn't know what to do!" Lori cried. "You were so excited about having a baby and it was a possibility that it was yours!"

Chase frowned. "What?"

Lori looked down. "I saw him a week before you came home."

"You gotta be kidding me!" Chase stood up. "You so fucking lucky my kids need a momma!" Lori huffed and kept her comment to herself. "Is this one mine? I'm getting a test as soon as that little nigga come out!"

Lori bit her lip and slowly nodded. "Fine."

"You damn right fine," Chase said. "I gotta deal with you and this nigga coming back from the dead."

"Technically…" Lori started. Chase cut his eyes at her and she closed her mouth. Chase rubbed his hands over his fade and stood up.

"I'll be back later."

Lori kept her mouth closed and held her breath until Chase closed the front door behind him. She heard her cell phone ringing somewhere in the kitchen so she went to find it. She rolled her eyes to see Tani was calling.

"What do you want?" Lori said. "Now is not a good time."

"Lori, I need you to call Meka and warn her!" Tani cried.

Lori frowned. "What's wrong? Why you sound like that?"

"Baby broke my arm! I'm on my way to the hospital but you gotta call and warn Meka. Baby has her address and she's going to her. She wants to kill her."

"Why would you give her the address? How do you have the real one?"

"Did you just hear what I said. That bitch kidnapped me from my job and beat me until I told her."

"Call the police!"

"And tell them what, Lori?" Tani cried. "Just do what I said. I don't have a number for Meka, we just had an address."

Lori nodded. "Okay, okay." Lori hung up and dialed the number Meka had been calling her from. She yelled in frustration when she heard the number was disconnected.

Cam frowned as Mia pushed pictures from magazines across the table.

"What?" Mia asked.

"Um, babe…these are…nice, but you sure you don't want to go with some fall colors?"

Mia frowned. "You don't like pastels?"

"Pastels are great," Cam said. "But not every pastel on the planet."

"I thought the rainbow theme was cute."

Cam bit her lip and shook her head. "No, babe. It's not."

Mia pouted and Cam turned the pictures over and scooted them to the end of the table. Mia sighed heavily.

"What am I going to do?"

Cam laughed. "First of all, calm down. I'm sure we'll find some nice colors."

"Maybe we should push the date back."

"You really want to be a virgin any longer than you need to?" Cam teased. Mia's eyes widened and Cam laughed. "I'm joking love, just calm down."

Mia began to eat the food in front of her while Cam pulled up pictures on her phone.

"Well, maid of honor, you need to get me together."

Cam smiled. "I was thinking, since your favorite color is orange…you could do teal and orange." Cam turned to show Mia the phone. "See?"

Mia's eyes lit up. "Camryn Charmaine, its perfect!"

"I know right? It'll be so cute."

"Oh, send me that picture so I can send it to Jeremiah," Mia said. Cam smiled and sent it to her. "Oh love, it's almost four, you gotta go get Ian."

"Oh, G's getting him today," Cam said, waving it off. Mia rose her eyebrow. "What?"

"Nothing."

Cam sighed. "What you wanna say, Mia?"

Mia held her hand up. "I'm staying out of your business, babe."

Cam rolled her eyes. "Yeah, okay."

Mia sucked her teeth. "I'm just saying, this all seems a little surreal don't you think?"

"Yes, it does, but I'm focused on what Ian needs and he needs a father."

"I get that Camryn, but…"

"Do you?" Cam asked, cutting her off. "Because I'm the single mother struggling to raise her son. I'm the one tired of being alone."

"What do you mean struggling? You aren't alone."

"You're right," Cam said. "Gino isn't dead, he's Ian's father and we are working on being a family. I know you never liked him…"

"Liked him, Camryn?" Mia interrupted. "He tried to have Ian killed! His psycho wife tried to kill you several times!"

"I know all of that! Mia, I do, but I can't harbor those feelings. I have to do what I think is best and I need you to support me on that, just like I've always supported you."

Mia sighed and threw her hands up in surrender. "Fine."

Cam smiled. "Thank you."

"But I do want to say one other thing."

"What is it?"

"You say things are different now, but be careful with that. Old habits die hard. You loved him hard, even after all he did…but don't forget who he was, Cam. Don't forget what he represented. If you truly believe that old Gino is gone…I'll support you 100 percent."

Cam looked at Mia and sighed. "Thanks."

Tameka pressed her fingers into her neck as she rolled her head around to relive some of the stress as she unlocked her front door. She had decided to work over that day since Marcus was taking an overnight shift but now she was truly regretting it.

She frowned when the alarm didn't sound, but then smiled, hoping Marcus had gotten home early.

"Baby?" she yelled, looking around the dark room. Tameka reached for a lap and turned the light on. She jumped when she saw someone sitting on her couch.

"How'd you know?" Baby said, smiling. She bit her lip, almost excited about the look on Tameka's face. "Oh, you have no idea how long I've waited to see that expression on your face." Baby laughed. "It was so worth it."

"What...how are you?" Tameka stuttered. "Hello, Baby."

Baby looked at her and laughed. "Hello, Baby? That's all you got, Tameka? Wow!" Baby stood up and Tameka backed up.

"What do you want?" Tameka asked, looking around.

Baby frowned. "What you looking for? Oh, probably that man of yours, huh?"

Tameka stopped looking around and glared at Baby. "What did you do?"

Baby licked her lips and twirled the gun in her hand around. "I could tell you, but then I'd have to kill you...oh wait! Gonna do that anyway."

Tameka swallowed the saliva in her mouth and tried to calm her heart. The feeling in the pit of her stomach let her know the outcome of this wouldn't be good.

"Where is he?" Tameka asked. "Marcus! Baby, can you hear me?"

Baby laughed. "Wanna try and find him? Go 'head. I'll allow it."

Tameka's fists balled at her side. She wanted to jump on Baby, but knew she'd have a bullet in her chest before she got close enough to do damage. Her focus had to be on Marcus. Maybe he was still alive, maybe he was still at work like he was supposed to be and Baby just wanted to see Tameka sweat.

Baby looked at her and sucked her teeth. "Ohhhhh, you think I'm bluffing." she said before smiling. "Guess you didn't come through the garage did you?"

Tameka started to run towards the kitchen to get to the garage door. She could hear Baby behind her laughing as she struggled with the locks to open it.

"Marcus! Baby, I'm coming!"

Tameka swung the door open and ran in, looking around to see if anything was out of place. Marcus' car was there but she didn't see him.

"Where is he!" Tameka screamed, turning around to look at Baby who was standing in the doorway. Tameka's heart thumped when Baby held up Marcus' car keys and hit the unlock button.

Tameka slowly turned towards his car. She felt her hands shaking as she walked towards the passenger door and grabbed the handle. His tint was dark so she couldn't see inside. Tameka knew she'd have to open the door to find out if he was inside or not.

"No!" she screamed. The blood on the driver's side window was the first thing she saw. Marcus' body was slumped over as blood poured from the side of his head. Tameka crawled into the passenger seat and grabbed him. "Baby, wake up. Come on, Marcus, wake up!"

She held him and cried. She knew Baby had done something, but seeing his lifeless body had broken her.

"It's a shame really," Baby said. "He actually forced my hand. I hadn't planned to kill him so soon."

She was leaning against the open door, looking in at Tameka with death in her eyes. Tameka looked over her shoulder while still holding her boyfriend's body and sighed.

"What was your plan?"

"For you to watch him die, just like you made me watch the love of my life die," she said in a slow, controlled tone. "See, for weeks, Gino has been racking his brain about if he could trust me to find you and figure out what happened that night, but I already knew what happened that night. You tricked me! You ripped my heart out and all I was trying to do, all me and Twan were trying to do was offer you a way out of your own hell. A hell you created because you were too stupid and too weak to leave a man who didn't love you!"

Tameka frowned. "Gino's dead."

Baby stopped ranting and stood up straight. "Nah, he's not," Baby said, clicking the gun at her side. "But you are."

Before Tameka could move, Baby shot her twice in the chest and closed the passenger door.

THIRTEEN

Gino huffed as he tried to call Baby again for the third time that week. He was getting more irritated by the minute, especially since he wasn't trying to show any irritation around Cam.

He dropped his phone on the couch when he heard a loud crash in the back.

"Ian, I told you to be careful!" Cam yelled. Gino frowned and got up to see what was going on. While he was walking, he heard a smack and Ian started crying. Gino jogged around the corner into his room. He pushed Cam back and picked Ian up to comfort him.

"What happened?"

Cam frowned. "Nothing happened, I'm disciplining my son."

"What did he do?" Gino said. He rubbed Ian's back and soothed him.

"Put him down, you can't do that after I spank him."

"Tell me what happened."

"I don't have to explain to you why I do what I do with my son!" Cam said, before storming out of the room. Gino watched her walk away, not sure what her problem was, before he went back to comforting Ian. Ian laid his head on Gino's chest and sobbed a little bit more before he calmed down and ended up sleeping. Gino put him in his bed before going to see what was up with Cam.

"Hey," he said, finding her in the kitchen in front of the sink. "What's your problem?"

"Nothing," she mumbled. "Just forget it."

He smirked. "Nah," he said while making her turn around. "You know better."

"Exactly!" Cam said, throwing her arms up. "I know better. I kept wondering when this little fairytale would end and I see now."

Gino frowned. "What are you talking about? You mad because I don't get why you whopped my son?"

"My son!" she yelled. "I've been raising him since he was born, I carried him while people tried to kill me and I decided to keep him when you didn't want him!"

Gino huffed, cracking his knuckles and trying to keep his opinion to himself.

"Go 'head."

"I've been doing this pretty well without you," Cam said. "I don't need you undermining me when I discipline him."

"You're right," he said, throwing his hands up.

Cam sighed. "Okay."

"Listen," he said. "You did do this on your own, but I'm here now." Gino stepped closer to her and grabbed her hands. "You gotta let me figure this out."

"G, it's not about you figuring this out. If we are going to be a family, we have to figure this out," she said, using her left hand to motion between the two of them. "I spanked him because he knows better than to push on that shelf like that and I told him to leave it alone before it fell. He could have gotten hurt if I didn't pull him back."

Gino nodded. "My bad."

"You can ask me stuff, but you didn't have to do all that."

"I said my bad."

Cam sighed. "Just forget it."

Gino watched her go back to washing dishes. He was confused on why she was still mad, but decided to leave it alone. He went back into the living room and sat down on the couch.

Her apartment was small. He was hoping she'd make up her mind about moving into the house he had waiting for them soon, because he was tired of being cramped up in that two-bedroom.

Granted, the house needed a little work. Gino wasn't pressed for cash, but the money that Tameka had taken out of all his accounts would definitely come in handy while taking care of a family.

"She better have my damn money," he mumbled. Gino scratched his nose before pulling his phone out to call Baby again. He mumbled a curse word when she didn't answer and threw his phone back down.

Cam came into the living room, but stood next to the couch.

"What's up?" he asked, hoping she didn't want to keep arguing.

"I'm going to run to the nail shop with Mia."

Gino nodded. "Alright."

Cam turned to walk off, but Gino grabbed her arm and pulled her down on his lap. She laughed but tried to move.

"Leave me alone," she said. Gino shook his head before holding her waist.

"Give me a kiss first."

Cam scrunched up her face and tried not to smile. "Nope, I don't like you."

Gino leaned in and kissed her anyway. "You love me girl, stop fronting."

She rolled her eyes and kissed him again before grabbing her purse and heading out the door.

Gino had finally relaxed on the couch, when his phone rang. Thinking it was Baby, he picked it up quick.

"Hey brother," Remy said. Gino sighed. "What you up to?"

"Chilling while my kid sleep. What's up, Rem?"

"Dang, what's wrong with you? Being a family man boring already?"

"Ha ha, nah….I just thought you were Baby."

Remy sucked her teeth. "You haven't talked to her either?"

"What you mean either? Y'all friends now?" Gino teased.

"Whatever, that last night we were in town, she took me to some bar…she ain't all that bad."

"Yeah well, I'm glad you wasted your time getting to know her."

"….."

"Remy, what? Why you quiet?" Gino asked. He could tell she was thinking about something.

"It may be nothing."

"Well, tell me anyway."

"When we were at the bar taking shots, Tati got this weird look in her eye. I tried to follow her path but I just saw some girl by the grill. I asked her what was up and she said nothing."

Gino sat up. "Why didn't you tell me before? What the girl look like?"

Remy sucked her teeth again. "I didn't think it was that deep," she said. "It wasn't Meka, I know what she looks like."

"What did she look like?" Gino repeated.

"She was short and slim and had some long, blonde ghetto ass braids."

"She a little darker than you?" Gino asked.

"Yeah!" Remy confirmed. Gino's temperature instantly went up. "Who was she?"

"The person who led Baby straight to Tameka," Gino said, looking around for his keys.

"What? Who was it?"

"Remember I told you about Meka's loud ass cousin who always got her into some mess?"

"The one who set her up to run Camryn off the road?"

"Right."

"Oh! I wish I would have known!" Remy yelled. "She's scan for not saying nothing! What you about to do?"

"Go back to town and find her," Gino said. "Can't believe I didn't think to look for her sooner."

"G!"

"What?" Gino asked, irritated that she'd yelled his name like that.

"Is Camryn there? You can't leave Ian by himself."

Gino froze in his place in the middle of the living room. "Shit…"

"Calm down," Remy coached him. "Where'd she go?"

"To the nail shop," Gino said, running his free hand down his face and sitting back down on the couch. He couldn't believe that he'd almost left his son home alone.

"Okay, well just chill out, think of a solid plan and I'll go see when the next train leaves."

Gino wanted to tell her not to go, but he wasn't thinking straight. He needed someone with him who was.

"Right," he said. "I'll meet you there."

When Gino finally got into Knoxville, he called Baywood to see if he knew where Tani stayed.

"Damn, I ain't even think about her," he said. Gino nodded, thinking the same thing. "I don't, but let me see if T does."

Gino waited while he heard Baywood ask his woman if he knew where Tani stayed. Gino smiled when she told Baywood that she did.

"I heard her," Gino said before Baywood could say anything.

"She ain't there though," Baywood said. "Shorty said she at her people's house on 3rd. Just got released from the hospital."

Gino rolled his eyes. "Baby got to her before I could."

"What?" Baywood asked. "Shorty crazy, watch out for her. You know she had Twan's nose wide open."

Gino's nose flared. "I'm already knowing."

"Well, let me know if you need me. Ain't much moving and Chase been wilin' since that shit happened."

"What he on?" Gino asked.

"Just acting up. Had to send his ass home the other day, was trying to camp out over here like he scared of that girl or something."

Baywood laughed but Gino just listened. Chase had tried him too many times since he'd been back and since he didn't care for Lori at all, he didn't care to hear about their problems.

"Aight, well let me go handle this."

"Right."

After Gino hung up, he made his way towards 3rd street to see about Tani and what she told Baby.

He laughed to himself when Scarface came through his speakers. Cam had talked him into buying some music service that played songs based on your likes. He wasn't really one for new music, so he had her program it to play 2Pac, Scarface, Do or Die and other old rap artists. She talked about him acting old, but once it started playing she knew most of the songs too.

Before Gino could get to Tani, he saw Chase running out of somebody's house.

"What is this dude doing?" Gino asked, watching him jump in his car and drive off. He was swerving and Gino knew he was either high or drunk, so he followed him.

About two streets over, Chase ran off the road and hit a pole. Gino slammed on his breaks and laughed in shock.

"What are the odds," he said, parking and getting out. He jogged over to the car and looked around to see if anyone was coming.

"You good?" he asked. Chase looked out the window and groaned.

"Get away from me, nigga," he slurred. Gino laughed.

"You sure? Look like you need help."

"Not from you nigga!" Chase spat. Gino smirked to see blood coming from his nose. "Bitch ass."

Gino shook his head. "You ain't gonna ever learn. I did you a favor by ratting on your baby momma. You killed the nigga that knocked her up and you still ain't grateful."

"I should kill you," Chase mumbled.

Gino scratched his nose and looked up at the night sky before reaching under his shirt for his gun. "You're right," he said before pointing it at Chase. "You probably should have."

Once the bullet pierced his head, Chase stopped struggling to get out the car and fell limp against the steering wheel. Gino looked at him for a second before tucking his gun back in his jeans and heading back to his truck.

Remy sent him a message that she was at the train station, so he drove off to get her. It only took him about ten minutes to get there.

"Have you talked to Tati?" she asked. Gino shook his head. "Well, I did."

"What she say?"

"I told her to meet us by her mom's house."

Gino smirked. "That was a good move."

"She was trying to act all cool, but I'm sure she knows that we know what she been up to."

Gino nodded. "I never liked her."

Remy sighed. "I know, but let's not jump to conclusions just yet, okay?" she asked, patting his shoulder. "We're almost done with this."

Gino sighed. "I just want my money."

"What?" Remy asked. "What money."

"Meka cleaned my accounts out before I had a chance to get back to them," he said. "I know that's what her ass living off of. Ain't no way she got a job."

"So you don't want her dead?" Remy asked. Gino laughed.

"Oh her ass is as good as dead," he said. "But I want my money first."

Remy nodded before sitting back in the passenger seat. "I'll text her and tell her we're on our way."

When they pulled up in front of Baby's mom's house, all the lights were out. Gino parked on the street, but him and Remy got out the truck. She leaned against the passenger side door while Gino stood in front of the truck. After a few minutes, Gino told Remy to call Baby but she didn't answer.

"Where the hell is this girl?" Gino said. Remy shrugged, but before she could respond, Baby walked around the corner.

"Calm down," she said. "I'm here, like I said I'd be."

"Cute cut," Remy said. Baby smirked and ran her hand over her new black, sleek bob.

"Thanks."

Gino frowned before looking at them both. "Y'all done?"

"Jeez, what's your problem?" Baby asked.

Gino's nose flared. "Stop playing with me, Tati. We know what you did to Tani. You know I don't like liars."

Baby sighed. "I didn't lie."

"You told me you didn't know that girl!" Remy snapped. Baby rolled her eyes before leaning against the fence of the court.

"Would you let me explain? Or are y'all just gonna yell at me all day?"

"Start talking."

Baby sucked her teeth. "I did see Tani in the bar that night," Baby said. "But I wasn't sure she knew where Tameka was."

"But you knew after you whooped her ass, right?" Gino asked. Baby looked at him for a second before nodding.

"I had an address, but since that failed before," Baby said, glancing at Remy. "I wanted to make sure it was legit before I got y'all involved in another wild goose chase."

Gino sighed. "So is it legit?"

"Yeah," Baby said, smiling. "I been up there, stayed a couple of days to make sure it was really her spot."

"Let's go," he said, throwing her the keys to his truck.

Baby's eyes widened. "Right now."

Remy smiled and walked around to the back door. "No time like the present."

"It's gonna take us a couple of hours to get there," Baby said. Gino looked at her and frowned. She sighed and took the keys to his truck and walked around to the driver's side.

When the finally got to Meka's neighborhood, Remy was in the back snoring and Gino was passed annoyed. It had taken them over three hours to get from Knoxville to Savanna. Meka always talked about getting a house in the suburbs when they first fell in love.

"This bitch," he mumbled. Baby frowned and looked at him. "I ain't talking about you."

"She on the next street over," Baby said. "But there's a problem."

Gino sighed in irritation. "What?"

"She got some dude, Marcus I think his name is."

"So?"

Baby sighed. "Gino this needs to be as clean and quick as possible. We can't have any surprises. I know where he works and what his car looks like, but I couldn't figure out his schedule."

Gino thought about it for a second before turning around and waking Remy up. He laughed at her confused expression before she realized what was going on.

"What's up?" she asked.

"I'm going to drop you and Baby off by Meka's house. I need y'all to get in and get her."

"What?" Remy asked. "What you mean? Where you going?"

"I need to peep a few things around here first, but I don't want to risk her leaving."

Remy nodded. Baby parked down the street from Meka's house, it was dark but street lights were on. "It's down on the right side."

Gino nodded. "Text me that info. I'll be back."

Baby smiled and nodded, pulling her phone out as she got out of the car.

While they were walking down the sidewalk, Remy noticed that Baby was smiling a little too hard.

"What's up with you?" Remy asked. Baby looked at her and frowned.

"Nothing. Just glad this is almost over."

Remy sighed. "Tell me about it." Baby nodded. "So you ain't run into Meka while you were here?"

Baby shook her head. "I stayed out of sight. Just wanted to make sure I ain't have to go kill Tani for giving me wrong info like Lori did you."

Remy smirked. "Yeah well, she probably wishes she was dead now."

"What you mean?"

Remy shook her head. "Nothing. Which house is it?"

"This one," Baby said, turning to walk through the grass. Remy pulled her back.

"What are you doing? Her car is in the driveway, you can't just walk up to the door."

Baby laughed. "Calm down girl, come on."

Remy watched Baby walk towards the side of the house and she frowned, wondering what was going on. She was tempted to call G back and tell him Baby was acting weird, but she just followed her to see what was going on.

"What the hell?" Remy asked when Baby pulled out a key to open the side door. "I thought you said you didn't see her."

"I lied," Baby said, pulling the door. "Come on. It's all good."

Remy sighed before following her into the dark garage. Baby switched the light on and Remy looked around and frowned.

"Where is she? In the house?" Remy asked. Baby smiled and shook her head before opening Marcus' car door. Remy looked inside and jumped back.

"You killed them both!" Remy yelled, looking wide eyed into the car. "He's going to flip!"

Baby laughed. "What's the problem? That's what he wanted."

"No, you idiot! We needed her!" Remy slammed the door and looked around. "I gotta figure something out before he gets back."

Baby frowned. "What are you talking about? Why did you need her?"

Gino had a bad feeling about this plan when he went past the address Baby gave him and no one was there. He called Remy's phone and she didn't answer, so he decided to go back to the house to make sure everything was cool and finish this once and for all.

Gino sighed when he noticed Cam was calling him back for the fourth time that hour. He slowed down and answered.

"Is everything okay?"

"Why haven't you answered?" she asked.

"I'm busy."

"Look, G, you can't just run off every time something doesn't go your way. How are we supposed to be a family like that?"

"Can't be a family if we live separately either," he mumbled.

Cam sighed. "We can get a place here. I didn't say I didn't want to be with you. I just don't see a valid reason to uproot and leave everything I've built here! I thought you'd understand that with our history."

Gino sighed. He knew exactly why Cam wasn't on board with moving. He was just hoping he could get her past it. He wanted to be home. He'd spent so much time away and missed out on a lot with his brother.

Gino was so sure that his whole plan was foul proof. Finding Tameka, getting his money back and making her pay for what she'd done and then finding Cam and his son and living happily ever after was like a hood fairy tale to him. It was how he'd be able to sleep at night and deal with his twin's death. The last couple of weeks had been revealing to Gino in a way he wasn't prepared for. From killing Chase, to Baby lying about knowing where Tameka was and now Cam telling him that she didn't want to move, Gino had never been so out of control in his life.

He didn't like it.

"We'll talk about this when I get home," he said. Cam got quiet for a second before she sighed.

"Okay....I love you."

"Love you, too," he said before hanging up quickly.

Gino ran his hands down his face before gripping his steering wheel and heading back to Meka's house. He tried to call Remy's phone again while speeding up.

Remy stopped moving when her phone rang. She cleared her throat before answering it. "Hey G."

"I'm outside. Y'all good?"

"...Yeah."

"...Rem, what's going on?"

She sighed. "Just come through the side door." Remy hung up and looked at Baby. "Listen to me. Did Tameka say anything about money or a safe in this house?"

"What?" Baby shook her head. "No! I didn't exactly give her a chance to talk about her finances."

Remy sucked her teeth. "You're so stupid!"

"Watch your mouth!" Baby said.

"It wasn't just about killing her, Tati!" Remy yelled. Baby just looked at her. "He wants his money."

"He never told me that."

"Because it wasn't for you to know! You were supposed to follow the plan."

They both turned and looked at the door when Gino walked in and froze. He pulled his shades off and smiled at them.

"What's up? Good news? Her car's here."

Remy looked at Baby and nodded her head towards Gino. Baby's eyes widened and she tried to shake her head without being obvious.

"What?" Gino asked.

Remy sighed when she figured out Baby wasn't going to say anything. She put her head down and opened the car door and stepped aside. Since it had been a few days since Baby shot Marcus and Tameka, the smell was beginning to take over the car. Gino frowned when it hit his nose before walking over and looking inside.

The last time he'd seen Tameka was the morning before he went to meet Camryn. That whole week, she had been running errands and offering to take money to the safe houses and doing everything a wife should. They hadn't been back from their honeymoon long, but Gino knew their love was different. It was obligated at that point. She felt he owed her and he had only married her to keep her away from Camryn and his son.

It wasn't always bad between them. When Gino first started out on the corner, Tameka was always around. She was always flirting and taking care of him. It wasn't a hard decision to keep her around, but somewhere along the lines he fell out of love.

And instead of her bowing out gracefully like a real woman, she'd tried sabotage his life and set him up to be killed. Tameka was the reason his money was gone. She was the reason his twin was dead. Gino wanted to watch her die.

"You had no right to kill her," he said, without taking his eyes off Tameka's body that was slumped over her dead lover.

"No right? She killed Twan in front of me!" Baby yelled. "You told me I could kill her! That was our deal."

"Nah," Gino said, turning around and moving into Baby's space. "Get me out of jail and I'll give you a front row seat to Tameka's death...ain't that what you said?"

Baby looked into the ice of Gino's eyes and a chill ran down her spine. "I...may have said that."

"G," Remy said, trying to calm him down.

"You had no right to kill my wife!" Gino yelled. Baby jumped at the sudden noise. All of the sudden, she stood up straight and held her head up.

"Well I did," she said. "Now what?"

"Oh shit," Remy mumbled when she saw the smirk on Gino's face. She backed up just as Gino's hands wrapped around Baby's throat.

She instantly began trying to scratch at any part of his flesh she could reach. Her eyes widened when he pressed his thumbs harder and lifted her off the ground. Her body landed on the pavement with a thud as he leaned over her body and tightened his grip. Gino smiled at the panicked look on her face.

"I never liked you," he whispered to Baby. "You turned my brother and my wife against me. You thought just because I got you out of jail that I'd let you slide for that shit?"

Baby's eyes watered as she fought to keep them open. She tried to look to Remy for help, but she just shook her head and looked away.

"G," Baby choked out, trying to pry his hands from her neck.

"You don't get to live after that," he said. "Tell Twan I'll see him in hell."

Remy ran her hands over her face as she saw Baby's body go limp and Gino finally let her throat go. "We need to go," she whispered.

"Nah, we gotta clean this up."

Remy's eyed widened. "Clean this up how? She did this."

Gino stood up straight. "But I did that," he said, pointing down to Baby's body. "I can't have my prints in here. Did you touch anything?" he asked.

Remy shook her head. "No."

Gino looked around the garage before pulling a pair of gloves out of his back pocket. "Good. Wrap her up in that tarp. I'll be back."

"Where you going!" Remy panicked. Gino started towards the door that led into the house.

"To find my money."

FOURTEEN

Cam rubbed Gino's back as he adjusted Ian in his arms and pointed down to Jean's tombstone.

"That's your uncle," he said. "I wish he could have met you. You would have loved him."

Cam stood next to Gino, unsure of what to say to comfort him. He had been back from Knoxville for a couple of days, but he was different. She wasn't sure what had happened, but he seemed a little calmer so she wasn't too worried.

She adjusted Ian's hat, glad that the weather was breaking and it would be warm soon. She couldn't believe that she had a one-year-old and that Gino was back in their lives. It still felt a little surreal, but now that she'd decided to move forward with their relationship on her terms, Cam felt better about it all.

Cam looked down at Gino's phone that was in her hand to see Granny Watson calling.

"You want me to answer?" she asked. Gino shook his head before kissing Cam's temple and turning away from his twin's grave.

"The food is probably done," he said.

"You sure you're ready to go?" Cam asked.

Gino nodded as Ian laid his head on his chest. Cam followed him back to the car and got in while Gino strapped Ian into his car seat.

While they were driving, Gino told Cam about a time Jean did something crazy and both of them got in trouble for it. She smiled, glad to see him thinking of good memories of his brother.

Cam frowned when she saw he missed the turn to go to Granny Watson's.

"Where we going?"

"Just up the street, real quick," he said, smiling at her. Cam's right eyebrow rose.

"What are you up to?"

"You'll see."

Gino pulled up to his vacant rental property and sighed. It was the house that he hoped to make his family's home. He'd done a lot of work on it and he was sure that if Cam gave it a chance, she'd love it. She was dead set on staying where she was and because he really needed his family to work, he'd play by her rules this time.

Cam told him about the money Meka gave her. He was upset that she'd kept it from him, but it did make him feel better about not being able to find his money at Meka's house. He knew she'd taken close to a million when she ran, knowing some of it went to his family eased the frustration a little. His plan was totally different now and not having control over every aspect of what happened had bothered him to some extent, especially when it came to Cam.

He realized, however, that it wasn't up to him. He wanted her to move on from their horrible past, but Gino finally figured out that he couldn't force that. Cam had to make that decision on her own.

"This is the house?" she asked. Gino nodded as Cam pointed out the window. "It has a for sale sign up."

He nodded again. "Someone actually put a bid in yesterday."

Cam looked at him for a moment. "You're selling it?" she whispered.

"We're selling it," he said. "We can't stay in that small ass apartment, but the money from this house will get us a decent house up there."

Cam's eyes watered up. "You serious?"

"That's what you want right?" he asked. Cam nodded and cried at the same time. "Well, why the hell you crying?"

She laughed through her tears. "Because, I can!" she said. Gino laughed at her and shook his head. "How much was the bid?"

"75."

"We can use that and some of the money I put up and get something real nice! We need at least three bedrooms."

Gino shook his head. "No."

"Why?" Cam asked, knowing what he was saying no to. "You made the money."

"We ain't using your money," he said. "Plus we don't need that many rooms right now."

Cam sighed and placed her hand on her belly. "Yes, we do."

Gino froze and looked at her. In that moment, he had deja vu. He remembered the moment Cam told him that she was pregnant with Ian and how mad he'd gotten. Gino felt guilt at his words, telling her to get rid of their child. He looked back at Ian, who was now sleep and thanked God that Cam was stubborn enough not to listen to him.

Cam's heart broke in the best way possible when she saw Gino's eyes water up at her news.

"That reaction is so much better than the last time I told you I was pregnant," she tried to joke, but her tears were clouding her own vision. Gino pulled her arm and leaned over the console to meet her in the middle. Cam groaned when he attacked her mouth with his own and her head begin to swim when both of his hands held her close to him.

"I love you so much right now," he said. Cam laughed and pulled back.

"You better love me so much for the rest of your life!"

Gino laughed before kissing her again and sitting back in his seat. He started the truck but then pulled her back to him for another kiss. Cam laughed before telling him to calm down.

He moved some hair from her face and pushed his forehead against hers.

This is what his peace finally felt like. All this time, he thought killing Meka and getting revenge for Jean's death was what he needed. Gino was wrong. His real revenge had turned out to be redemption from the one he loved the most.

Nothing would be better than that.

www.ingramcontent.com/pod-product-compliance
Lightning Source LLC
Chambersburg PA
CBHW071355250626
47159CB00004B/1626